Alan Gibbons is a primary school teacher and
started writing children's books in 1990. His
central themes come from his own experience, and
observation of children. Alan Gibbons lives in
Liverpool with his wife and four children.

Twin Strikers

Alan Gibbons

A Dolphin
Paperback

First published in Great Britain in 1999
as a Dolphin paperback
by Orion Children's Books
a division of the Orion Publishing Group Ltd
Orion House
5 Upper St Martin's Lane
London WC2H 9EA

A catalogue record for this book
is available from the British Library
Typeset by Deltatype Ltd, Birkenhead, Merseyside
Printed in Great Britain by Clays Ltd, St Ives plc

ISBN 1 85881 568 1 (pb)

Rough Diamonds

THE SQUAD

Darren 'Daz' Kemble (goalkeeper)
Joey Bannen (defence and substitute goalkeeper)
Mattie Hughes (defence)
Anthony 'Ant' Glover (defence)
Jimmy Mintoe
Carl Bain (defence)
John O'Hara (mid-field)
Jamie Moore (mid-field)
Kevin 'Guv' McGovern (mid-field)
Bashir Gulaid (mid-field)
Pete 'Ratso' Ratcliffe (mid-field)
Dave Lafferty (striker)
Gordon Jones (striker and captain)

Manager: Ronnie Mintoe

PART ONE

Coming Apart

As a successful team you are going to have unsuccessful periods as well. It's how you cope with those.

Denis Irwin,
Manchester United and
Ireland defender.

One

Kev McGovern settled himself on the patchwork of mud and yellowing grass that made up Jacob's Lane playing fields and frowned. The wind-swept sports ground was no Theatre of Dreams, but the matches that took place every Sunday morning on its six pitches were Kev's obsession. He had his heart set on the South Sefton Junior League championship and his team-mates were letting him down. He was the team captain, the Guv'nor. Except that he hadn't governed a single thing that morning. The Rough Diamonds had put on a sluggish display in the first half against Fix-It DIY. Kev looked up expectantly at the approach of the Diamonds' manager, Ronnie Mintoe. Maybe he could inject some life . . .

'Look lads,' Ronnie was telling his dispirited troops as they gathered for the half-time pep talk under a leaden February sky. 'You've got to kill them off. I really mean it, go for the jugular. You've had enough chances to win this match three times over. Honestly, one-one at half-time is a travesty. We must have had seventy per cent of the possession.' Discovering that his words were falling on deaf ears he took a deep breath. 'Have a heart. It's no fun being a manager. Can you imagine what it's been like for me watching? Frustrating isn't the word for it. Come on lads. Play as a team. You don't want me to burst a blood vessel, do you?'

The attempt at humour was lost on the Diamonds. They were wet through from the morning rain, plastered with mud, and down in the mouth about their masterpiece of underachievement in the first half.

'We need more movement,' said Kev, adding his two-pennyworth. 'And the passing's got to improve. Do you realize how many times we gave the ball away?'

'No,' grunted Conor sarcastically. 'But I'm sure you're going to tell us.'

'Don't you ever listen to anybody?' demanded Jamie. 'You might just learn something for once. I can't remember the last time you got the ball through to me.'

Always master of the flip reply, Conor was ready. 'I can't pass to you if you're not up with the play. You know what, I think you're getting a bit of a belly on you, lardy-boy. You need to look at your fitness level.'

'And you need to look at your mouth,' Jamie retorted angrily, though not before trying to suck in a non-existent spare tyre. 'Before I fill it with my fist.'

Conor's twin brother Liam winced at the exchange. Why couldn't Con just try to fit in?

'That,' said Ronnie pointedly, 'is exactly what I'm on about. You two are supposed to be our strike force. *On strike* is more like it. You've got to learn to play for each other.'

'Tell him that,' said Jamie. 'Everything was all right until he got into the team.'

'Enough!' snapped the usually placid Ronnie. 'You ought to be able to beat this lot in your sleep. Have you forgotten our last meeting with Fix-It . . .?'

He didn't finish the sentence. Soccer mastermind Ratso was on hand to provide the match statistics. 'We tanked them,' he said, 'six-nil.'

'And,' said Ronnie stabbing an accusing finger at Conor and Jamie, 'four of the goals came from you two.'

'To be exact,' Ratso interjected helpfully, 'Jamie got one and Conor got a hat-trick.'

'Too right,' said Conor, giving Jamie a smug glance. 'Good performance, wasn't it?'

'So get your act together,' said Ronnie. 'You've got to beat teams like Fix-It if you want to win the championship. And that,' he added with extra emphasis, 'is non-negotiable.'

But as Kev led the Diamonds back onto the pitch he knew that the team talk had done nothing to cure their problems. Not only were Conor and Jamie glaring at each other, Joey Bannen was airing his grievances to fellow substitute Chris Power. 'Ronnie wants to look at the left flank,' he was saying. 'Bashir needs some service.' He glanced across at Liam. 'And he isn't getting it.'

Kev shook his head. Talk about sour grapes. Joey hadn't let up on Liam since he'd lost his place to him two months before. What made things worse was the fact that big Daz Kemble, the Diamonds' goalkeeper, was Joey's best mate and was also giving Liam the cold shoulder. Just lately the squad had had more vendettas than a Sicilian village, and most of them revolved around the twins.

'Ready boys?' asked the referee.

'Ready as we'll ever be,' replied a discouraged Kev McGovern.

The second half followed a similar pattern to the first with both teams packing the mid-field and squandering possession like they were registered charities.

'What the flipping heck do you call that?' demanded Conor angrily as Jamie sliced the ball out of play. Jamie simply ignored him.

'We're going to have to do something about those

two,' said Ratso. No sooner were the words out of his mouth than Liam missed his tackle on the Fix-It number seven, provoking mocking laughter from Joey Bannen. 'And those two,' sighed Ratso.

Emboldened by their opponents' fitful performance, Fix-It started to put pressure on the Diamonds back four. Daz was fortunate to beat out one particularly rasping shot for a corner. 'That's the area you're supposed to cover,' Daz yelled as Liam took the near post. 'Our goal was left completely exposed. So where were you?'

'Stranded upfield,' Liam explained. 'Me and Bashir got overcommitted. I didn't expect our attack to break down that quickly.'

'Well you should,' said Daz dismissively. 'It's called reading the game. Don't do it again, right?' Liam ignored the comment and concentrated on defending the corner. As it turned out it was a poor one and slapped harmlessly into the side netting. 'Danger over,' said Daz, placing the ball for a goal kick. 'No thanks to you, Savage.'

Liam turned at the edge of the area. 'What *is* your problem?' he asked. 'What have I ever done to you?'

Daz didn't even reply. His kick soared down the field, almost into the opposing penalty area. 'You've heard of wind-assisted,' Ratso confided in Kev. 'Well, that was temper-assisted. Daz hasn't half got it in for Liam.'

'Tell me about it,' said Kev ruefully. He could see the double receding before his eyes. The game stuttered on scrappily until five minutes from the end, when Fix-It drove forward in force.

'Get in a tackle,' roared Kev. 'Won't *somebody* get in a tackle?'

It was Gord who responded first, rushing Fix-It's barrel-chested striker Colin Hooper. In a full-blooded challenge Gord would always come off worst. He crashed heavily to the ground and immediately clutched his shoulder. Hooper didn't so much as break his stride. Looking up, he beat the advancing Daz Kemble with a looping lob. Two-one to Fix-It.

'Great,' said Kev. 'Absolutely rotten wonderful.'

But going behind wasn't the Diamonds' only concern. 'Hang on a minute,' shouted Ant Glover, Gord's partner in the centre of the defence. 'I think Gord's hurt.' Gord was sprawled full length on the turf, still holding his shoulder.

'How does it feel?' asked Ronnie.

'Painful,' croaked Gord. 'Really painful.' As Ronnie and Ant helped Gord off the field, the Diamonds' substitutes started warming up expectantly.

'You're on, Chris,' shouted Ronnie. 'You know where I want you. Go straight into central defence.'

Joey stared in disbelief. 'I don't believe it,' he said. 'Overlooked again.'

'Come off it,' said Dougie Long, the third sub. 'You don't see too many dwarves playing centre half. The average worm could jump higher for a header.'

Joey scowled. He was sensitive about his size. 'And you don't see many retards playing in any position,' he shot back.

Kev shook his head. The Diamonds were showing all the togetherness of a nest of vipers. 'Come on, lads,' he shouted, clapping his hands. 'We've got less than five minutes to turn this game round.'

The prospect of being beaten by second-to-bottom Fix-It finally kick-started the Diamonds. Both Bashir and Kev made promising runs into the box before losing possession, but it was a drive from outside the area by Jamie that gave the Diamonds their opening. The shot forced one of the Fix-It centre halves to head the ball out for a corner. Jimmy Mintoe took it, bending the ball just out of the reach of the Fix-It keeper. Conor was first to react. Rising above the marking defender he headed it powerfully inside the near post. Two-all.

'Yes,' said Kev, thrusting his clenched fists skyward. Only Jamie showed little interest at the equalizer. 'Lighten up,' said Kev. 'Conor is on our side, you know.'

'Could have fooled me,' said Jamie. The referee blew the final whistle less than a minute later.

'Two-all,' said Ratso philosophically. 'Could have been worse.'

'Could have been better too,' observed Kev. 'A lot better.' The draw had only come at a price. Gord was still receiving attention for his injury on the touch-line, and was in obvious discomfort. Meanwhile, the warring members of the team were giving each other the cold shoulder as they left the pitch.

'I'm sure things will improve,' said Ratso.

'Too right,' said Kev, indicating the hostile glances being exchanged between Liam and Joey and Conor and Jamie. When you've just introduced twins into the team and nobody gets on with them, you've got double trouble. 'It'll improve all right – just as soon as we sort that lot out.'

Two

Liam joined the crowd of Diamonds surrounding Gord.

'It doesn't look too good,' said Ronnie. 'I'm going to run him up to the hospital. You know, just in case.'

'Are you OK, Gord?' asked Kev, as Ronnie led Gord towards his car. Gord nodded, but the pain showed on his face. 'We could have done without that,' Kev murmured. 'Central defence is one place we have been performing. We don't want to lose Gord.'

'Defenders are two-a-penny,' said Conor coolly. 'It's strikers who win games.' Liam shook his head. Sensitive his brother wasn't. It had always been like this. Liam the serious one who worked hard in school, Conor the lippy one who fancied himself as some sort of superscally. They didn't have a single thing in common, except a birthday. Oh, and football of course.

Kev spoke for the whole team as he buttonholed Conor. 'Is that all you can say? Gord isn't just a two-a-penny defender. He's a mate, and the sooner you understand that the better.'

'Touchy,' said Conor.

If he was expecting sympathy from Liam he was in for a disappointment. 'You don't get it, do you Con?'

'What's to get?' asked Conor. 'He got a knock. He'll live.'

'Oh, do shut up,' said an exasperated Liam.

Conor wasn't as bad as the rest of the Diamonds thought. He could be generous and caring. The trouble was, he knew how to hide it. That Sunday morning, he was hiding it really well!

'Shut up yourself,' said Conor, over-reacting as usual. 'Who do you think you're talking to?' The argument was cut short when the Liver Bird arrived. The Diamonds and the Liver Bird were the two teams on the giant Diamond estate, but there was no love lost between them. They were two tribes always on the verge of going to war.

'What's this, Diamonds?' asked Luke Costello, the Liver Bird captain and Kev's arch-enemy. 'Slipped up again, I hear?'

'Then you heard wrong,' Kev told him. 'We drew.'

'Against Fix-It?' snorted Andy 'Brain Damage' Ramage. 'I don't think that's much to boast about. Bottom, aren't they?'

'Next to bottom,' Chris Power informed him irritably.

'A draw against the next-to-bottom side,' said Costello sarcastically. 'Impressive, eh?' His comment drew appreciative laughter from the rest of the Liver Bird team.

'So how did you do?' asked Conor. Liam winced again as Conor swallowed the bait.

'Won, of course,' Brain Damage replied. 'Four-one against Sefton Dynamoes. That puts a bit of space between us, doesn't it? Four points, on my reckoning.'

Liam looked round for Ratso. He'd be sure to know the placings. But he was nowhere to be seen.

'Bit of a turn-up, eh McGovern?' said Costello. 'A new team like us showing you the way. What was it you wanted to be? Oh yes, the new Brazil. Funn-ee. We could teach you a thing or two.'

'We've nothing to learn from you lot,' Kev answered sharply. 'Only how to collect more bookings than the Spice Girls. You're a bunch of boot boys, and that's all.'

'Boot boys who are four points ahead of you in the table,' said Brain Damage smugly.

'Not for long,' said Conor, earning himself a gale of raucous laughter.

'Dream on Diamonds,' said Costello by way of a parting shot. 'Dream on.'

'I should have popped him one,' said Conor. Liam pursed his lips and shook his head. 'What's with you?' asked Conor.

'You're an embarrassment, Con,' said Liam. 'Pop him one. Is that your answer to everything?'

'I'm with Conor,' said Chris. 'We shouldn't let them get away with it. They need putting in their place.'

'And fighting isn't the way to do it,' said Kev.

There was a stunned silence. They weren't the words you expected from the Guv'nor. He usually lashed out first and asked questions later.

'Did I hear you right, Guv?' asked Jamie Moore.

'You heard,' Kev answered. 'It's time we used our heads instead of our fists. If we're going to turn this season round we need some self-discipline. Remember what happened to England when David Beckham lost it against Argentina. We'll get nowhere letting the likes of Costello and Brain Damage get under our skin.'

'What's this, Guv?' asked Conor. 'Going soft?'

'If you'd been round for more than a couple of months,' Jamie told him, 'you wouldn't even ask.'

Conor wasn't impressed. 'Who gave you the right to order everybody about anyway?'

'We all did,' Jimmy Mintoe told him. 'He's the captain, the Guv'nor.'

'On the pitch maybe,' said Conor, refusing to back down. 'But nobody's telling me I can't put clowns like them in their place.' He indicated the Liver Bird as they filed into the changing rooms.

'I hate to admit it,' said Ant, 'but I'm with Conor. We're letting them get away with murder.'

'And I'm with Guv,' said Liam with as much force as

he could muster. 'They're trying to get us rattled and you're daft enough to let them.'

'Brotherly love, eh?' chuckled Joey Bannen, keen to score points off Liam.

'An uneasy silence followed, broken by Ratso's voice. 'Like to see the new table, lads?' he asked.

'Why, where've you been, Rats?' asked Kev.

'Collecting the results,' Ratso replied. 'It makes grim reading.' He handed Kev the hastily scribbled league table.

'Grim is right,' said Kev. He returned the scrap of paper to Ratso and Ratso relayed it to the team:

	Pl	W	D	L	Pts
Longmoor Celtic	13	9	4	0	31
Ajax Aintree	13	9	3	1	30
Liver Bird	13	8	3	2	27
Northend United	13	7	3	3	24
St Patrick's Thistle	13	7	3	3	24
Rough Diamonds	13	7	2	4	23

'Four points adrift of the Liver Bird,' said Jimmy.

'And eight points off the top,' said Kev, the information hitting him like a slug in the belly.

'You know why,' said Conor.

'No,' said Kev. 'I don't, but I'm sure you'll tell me.'

'It looks obvious to me,' said Conor. 'When I agreed to play for you in the summer I thought you could handle yourself. You go round saying you're the Guv'nor, but now you tell us we can't put Costello and Brain Damage in their place. We're letting teams walk all over us. The Diamonds are going soft.'

'Don't talk such rubbish,' said Ratso. But as Liam

looked round the players he could see the doubt in their faces. Conor had struck a chord.

Liam and Conor were met at the door by their mother.

'OK,' she said, hands on hips, 'so whose turn was it to put the bikes in the shed?'

'You mean they were left out again?' Liam asked. He was genuinely surprised. He'd even reminded Conor. It was always the same. He took his responsibilities seriously. Unlike Conor.

'Yes they were left out,' Mum replied. 'So whose turn was it?'

The reply came in stereo. 'His.' Liam and Conor were pointing at each other.

'That's four hundred quids' worth of bikes,' said Mum. 'And you leave them out on the lawn. As if that's not enough, you left the shed door wide open. All your dad's tools are in there. Why don't you just put up a sign: *Steal me.*'

'OK Mum,' drawled Conor. 'Don't go on. We get the message.'

'No,' said Mum, her eyes narrowing. 'I don't think you do. Do you know how hard your dad and I have to work to buy you things . . .?'

The sermon was interrupted as Dad made an appearance. He made his usual laid-back contribution. 'Oh, give it a rest, Karen. Lads will be lads. Didn't you ever do anything wrong when you were young?'

'Yes,' she answered, annoyed that he hadn't backed her up. 'But I didn't keep on doing it. Mind you, I'm not a *lad.*'

Dad watched her stamp angrily into the living room. 'Ouch,' he said. 'Not the right thing to say, was it?'

'No,' said Conor, winking. 'You broke the parents' united front.'

The pair of them joined in conspiratorial laughter. Liam stood apart. Funny how they always stuck together. It had always been like that, Dad and Conor. They were more like buddies than father and son. *They* should have been the twins. Liam was more like Mum, hardworking and serious. Liam could just imagine Conor following in Dad's footsteps. And what footsteps they were. He mentally listed Dad's impressive cv. Former boating lake attendant, tea bag perforator and toilet factory labourer. He'd been a blower-off in the bidet department! What was it next? Oh yes, glass washer, club doorman and stand-up comic. He hadn't been much good at any of them, but at least he met Mum working in the club. There had even been a short spell as a professional wrestler. Johnny Arapaho, he'd been called. He used to arrive home with an American Indian head-dress and enough bruises to paint the kitchen blue. Losing to the Salford Mauler was the final straw. After that, he hung up his shorts. That was typical. He never seemed to hold any one job down for long. For the last eighteen months he'd been a market trader. Which explained why half the living room was occupied by stock. His van had been broken into a few months previously, so nothing was kept in it overnight any more.

'Anyway,' Dad whispered. 'You can tell me. Who did leave the bikes out?'

'Me,' admitted Conor with a disarming grin.

'I knew it,' said Dad. 'I was just the same when I was a lad.' Liam pulled a face. How did Conor do it? He'd turned leaving the shed door open into a badge of honour. He could wriggle out of first-degree murder, if he wanted. 'Oh, look at old sourpuss,' said Dad. 'Lighten up, Liam. You'll crack that face if you don't watch. Smile, why don't you?'

But Liam was in no mood to smile. He glared at Conor. 'Maybe he doesn't give me much to smile about,' he snarled.

'Been arguing again, eh?' said Dad. 'Well, that's what brothers are for.' With that, he slipped into the living room to appease Mum.

'Why didn't you own up to Mum?' asked Liam.

'Because, lame brain,' Conor retorted, 'she would have grounded me. Du-uhh.'

'That's typical of you,' said Liam. 'Nothing matters, does it? Just so long as Conor's OK.'

'Meaning?'

'Meaning you don't care about anyone but yourself. You never give anybody else a moment's thought. Like at the match. You couldn't care less how Gord was.'

Conor yawned. 'He'll be all right. Besides, if he can't stand the heat he should stay out of the kitchen.'

Liam gave a cry of exasperation.

'And you can cut that out, Liam,' snapped Mum as she emerged from the living room. Liam saw Conor smirking. The injustice of it! For the second time that day he could have strangled his twin

Three

Sort it out. Easier said than done. That two-all draw, it was the pits. I was embarrassed to be part of it. The day the Diamonds won the Challenge Cup last year I thought all our troubles were over. We were improving with every game

towards the end of last season. I couldn't wait for the next one to start. One big push and we were bound to take the title. But just lately everything's started to go pear-shaped for us. I don't get it. Back in October we were sitting pretty in fourth place in the league, well positioned for a push for the title. We even strengthened our side with the addition of the twins, Liam and Conor Savage. But somehow by strengthening the side, we've ended up weakening it. Suddenly we're in sixth place and sliding. With Gord injured, our problems are piling up. Even my worst enemies, a bunch of cloggers who call themselves the Liver Bird have moved above us. Confused? Me too. The Savage twins might be terrific players but their arrival seems to have upset the balance of the whole team. The signings who were supposed to be the solution to our difficulties have turned out to be part of the problem. They'd hardly pulled their boots on before there were all sorts of arguments and rumours and sly comments. And when the twins aren't squabbling with the rest of the squad they're scrapping with each other! I thought me and our Gareth were bad, but those two! No doubt about it, the Diamonds aren't a happy outfit any more. Honestly, what do I have to do get somewhere?

My life got off to a lousy start when Dad cleared off for four whole years, leaving Mum to bring up me and Gareth. When he came back, things got even worse. Dad turned out to be the right-hand man of a disgusting piece of work by the name of Lee Ramage, one of the biggest villains in the north end of Liverpool. Hardly what I'd been dreaming about all the while he was away.

Anyway, football's meant to be my escape route out of all that, my crusade, the way to sort myself out. Now even that's turning out to be as messed up as everything else. I've got to turn things round. And I will, even if it kills me!

Four

It was Saturday night almost a week later and this time Kev was fuming. For once it wasn't the state of the Diamonds, it was his kid brother Gareth. He was going to spoil his sleep-over at uncle Dave and aunty Pat's.

'Have we got to share with him?'

The *we* was Kev and Chris. Sharing with your little brother was so uncool. Kev's Diamonds' team-mate Chris Power was in foster care with Kev's uncle and aunty, but he was still finding his feet in the Tasker household. No matter how often Kev looked at him expecting moral support, Chris hung back. He wasn't about to rock the boat in his new home.

'Gareth'll spoil our fun.' Kev ranted on. 'Why's he got to be in *our* room.'

'Because,' Mum informed him sharply, 'you, Chris and Gareth are boys . . .'

Kev glared at his little brother imagining horns and a forked tail. 'In his case,' he seethed, 'that's a matter of opinion.'

'And,' Mum continued, none too pleased at being interrupted, 'you can't expect Cheryl to share with a boy.'

Cheryl wrinkled her nose in mock distaste.

'He's got smelly feet,' said Kev.

'So,' said Gareth indignantly, 'you've got . . .' He was stuck for a reply. '. . . A smelly head.'

'Oh, that really makes sense,' sneered Kev.

'Come on now,' said uncle Dave. 'I'm sure we can work this out. Tonight ought to be an adventure.'

If this is an adventure, thought Kev, then Uncle Dave's led a sheltered life. 'I have slept-over before, you know,' he said.

'I've got a video out,' said uncle Dave.

'What is it?' Gareth asked eagerly.

'Sorry lad,' said uncle Dave. 'It's a 15 certificate. Too old for you, I'm afraid.'

'But Kev and Cheryl aren't fifteen!' Gareth protested. 'Or Chris.' The six-year-old was burning with injustice. He was building up to a major temper fit.

'Nearly,' said Kev. 'And anyway, you have to go to bed early.'

'Can't I stay up?' asked Gareth pleadingly, suspending his tantrum for a moment.

'No, you can't,' said Mum. 'It's a school day tomorrow.'

'I hate school,' huffed Gareth, slipping back easily into his angry mode.

'No, you don't,' said Mum.

'Yes I do.'

Mum gave Kev a disapproving look. 'I can guess where he got that attitude from.'

Kev threw up his arms in exasperation. 'I don't believe it,' he said. 'Gareth gets in a nark, and I get it in the neck!'

'Come with me, Gareth,' said Cheryl, always the peacemaker, 'We've got toffee ice-cream.'

As Gareth allowed himself to be led into the kitchen, Kev exchanged glances with uncle Dave. *Why didn't I think of that?* their expressions were saying. 'This is really good of you, Dave,' said Mum. 'I haven't had a night out for ages.'

'Forget it,' said Dave.

'Forget what?' asked aunty Pat, making her entrance.

—— 18 ——

Kev looked at Mum and her twin sister. They were very alike, except for one major difference; Mum looked five years older. Something to do with smoking, but more to do with marrying Dad.

'I was just thanking Dave for minding the boys,' said Mum.

'No need,' said aunty Pat. 'He wants us out of the house so he can watch that Arnold Schwarzenegger movie. Big kid.' Dave grinned sheepishly.

'Where are you going?' asked Kev, running his eyes over Mum and aunty Pat. They looked different in their black dresses and make-up.

'We're meeting some mates,' said aunty Pat, applying a final layer of lipstick. 'Then we're off clubbing it.'

'What,' Kev chuckled, 'dancing?'

Aunty Pat did a wiggle. Chris laughed. Kev covered his face with his hands. 'Got it in once.' Kev opened his palms and grimaced. 'Cheeky little so-and-so,' said aunty Pat.

'It's hard to imagine, that's all,' said Kev. 'I mean, you're both . . .' How do I put this? he thought.

'Old?' Mum volunteered.

Kev pulled a face. 'Well, yes.'

'You're never too old,' said aunty Pat skittishly.

'I don't know,' said Mum, brushing back her hair, 'I feel it sometimes.'

Kev felt guilty. She'd been in such a good mood, and he'd spoilt it. He knew exactly what she was thinking. Eight years with Dad, then another four bringing up two boys on her own. It was enough to make anybody feel old.

'Hang on,' said aunty Pat. 'Listen, that's our taxi.' She gave uncle Dave a peck on the cheek, then called to

Cheryl in the kitchen. 'We're off kids. See you in the morning.'

'Have a nice time,' shouted Cheryl.

Kev listened to the taxi pulling away and grimaced again. Why didn't he ever think of saying anything like that?

'Your mum looked nice,' said Chris. 'Different.' Kev knew what he meant. She'd been slopping round so long in those washed-out jeans and shapeless tops, it was like they were painted on.

Uncle Dave broke in on the conversation. 'Shall I put the video on?' he asked.

'Give it a few minutes,' said Kev. 'Just till Gareth goes up.'

'Oh yeah,' said Dave. 'I forgot.'

'Does aunty Pat ever do this for you?' asked Chris.

'What's that?' asked uncle Dave.

'Stay in while you go out on your own,' Chris explained. 'I've never seen you go out with any of your mates, that's all.'

'Haven't got any,' laughed Dave. 'No seriously, it's not my scene. I'd rather stay home and watch the box. I'm not much of a drinker and I don't like clubs. I can't dance. Two left feet, that's me.'

'So where did you meet aunty Pat?' asked Kev.

'You'll laugh,' said uncle Dave.

'No, we won't,' said Chris. 'Go on, where?'

'I tipped her into the park lake.'

'You what?'

'She was getting out of a rowing boat at the Botanic Gardens in Southport. I tried to help her out and ended up capsizing the boat.'

'You never!'

Dave grinned. 'I did.'

'And she still went out with you?'

Dave pointed at the wedding photo on the shelf over the TV. 'Looks like it.'

They were still laughing when Cheryl and Gareth walked in. 'What's up with you three?' asked Cheryl.

'I was just telling them how I met your mum,' said uncle Dave.

'Oh, the rowing boat,' Cheryl yawned.

'Why?' asked Gareth. 'What happened?'

'I'll tell you on the way upstairs,' said Cheryl.

'I can go by myself,' Gareth protested.

'But aunty Carol told me to make sure you brush your teeth,' said Cheryl.

Gareth scowled and stamped upstairs. 'I hate being the youngest,' he grumbled.

'Yiss!' said Kev. 'That's the pain out of the way. Put the video on.'

Just as the film was about to start, Cheryl reappeared munching crisps. She perched on the arm of Kev's chair. 'Didn't your mum look great?' she said. 'You never know, she might cop off tonight.'

Kev's face drained of blood. What did she have to say that for?

Five

Liam had been trying to shift Conor from the Gamestation for half an hour. 'Come on, Con,' he pleaded. 'If we don't make a move soon, we'll be late for the training session.'

Conor glanced at the clock on his bedside table.

'We'll be all right. It only takes five minutes to ride up to South Road.'

'Ten, more like,' said Liam.

'And we've got half an hour,' said Conor. 'Honestly, it's the same every Monday evening. Take it easy, why don't you?'

'You know how much I hate being late,' said Liam.

'And you know how much I hate being rushed,' Conor retaliated. There was the hint of a smile playing on his lips. Conor loved getting Liam on edge. It was another of the ways he took after Dad. Only Mum was the one *he* wound up. 'How's about one more race?'

Liam eyed the Gamestation warily. 'There isn't time.'

Conor laughed. 'Of course there is.'

'OK,' Liam agreed reluctantly. 'One game.'

'I'm having the yellow car,' said Conor, grabbing a control pad. 'It's the fastest.'

'No, it isn't,' said Liam. 'They're all the same.'

'So how come I always win?'

'Not always you don't.'

'Well, mostly then.'

'Oh, I don't know,' said Liam watching the time clicking by on Conor's digital alarm. 'Let's get on with it. I'll have red.'

Conor chuckled. 'Red, red, I'd rather be dead.'

Liam frowned his disapproval. 'Just start the game.' As the two cars tore away from the starting line, Liam felt the tension rising. Conor was right; he usually did win. That's why Liam was so reluctant to play. But why? What made him so much better? After all, they were identical twins. Liam was older too, if only by five minutes.

'Yes,' said Conor. 'First into the chicane.'

Liam felt the little hairs prickling on the back of his neck. He'd love to win a game for once, just like he'd like to score more goals on the football field. He was way better than Conor at school, but somehow, being better at English, Maths and Science wasn't half as exciting.

'Want me to wait for you, Liam?'

'Just play, will yer?' hissed Liam, irritated by Conor's cockiness, but even more so by his own poor handling of his car. He glimpsed the clock. They were never going to make it to South Road on time.

'Oh, this is too easy,' crowed Conor. 'What's up, Liam, finding it hard to concentrate?'

Liam stared at the monitor screen. He'd crashed into a boulder. OK, so it was a virtual boulder, but it still hurt. 'Rats.' He reversed quickly and pursued the yellow car at breakneck speed. He glanced at the lap counter. Half a kilometre behind Conor.

'Last lap,' said Conor. 'Follow me home, loser.'

Liam tried to cut the next corner and clipped the stone wall. He watched in anguish as the red car went spinning out of control. By the time he'd manoeuvred the car out of the lake and back onto the road, Conor was out of sight.

'Home straight,' crowed Conor. 'Sure you don't want me to wait for you?'

'Oh, shut up Conor.'

'Sore loser,' said Conor, a mischievous glint in his eye. 'Anyway, I've crossed the line. Game over.'

Liam watched the hated words CONOR WINS flash across the screen and tossed the control pad onto the table. 'So we can go now?'

'One more game?' asked Conor. It wasn't a serious suggestion, just his usual wind-up.

'You promised,' said Liam, struggling to hide the whine in his voice.

'OK, OK, we'll go.'

'Late again, lads,' said Ronnie, tapping his watch.

Liam glared angrily at Conor, then turned to Ronnie. 'Sorry.'

'It's only five minutes,' said Conor. Apologies weren't his style.

'Ten, more like,' said Kev.

'Anyway,' said Ronnie. 'We're looking at our movement off the ball. It was our biggest problem against Fix-It.'

Liam wasn't so sure. There was the little matter of team spirit. There wasn't any.

'Look lads,' Ronnie continued, warning to his theme.'We can't just stand there watching the man on the ball do his stuff. One good run off the ball can pull a defender out of position.'

'As if we didn't know that already,' Conor whispered to Liam. Liam ignored him.

'That's what I want to see from our front players. You in particular, Jamie and Conor. The more you change position, the more you disconcert the opposition defence.'

'Tell me something I don't know,' said Conor. The last time he listened to advice, dinosaurs walked the Earth. 'I don't just stand there, you know.'

'You did against Fix-It,' said Ronnie. 'Especially when Jamie had the ball.' Conor gave a little shake of the head.

'I don't know what you're shaking your head for,' Liam said. 'Ronnie's right.'

'Whose side are you on?' asked Conor.

'The team's.' Liam ran his eyes over the team. No Gord.

'Right,' said Ronnie. 'Just in case you're wondering, Gord's shoulder is really sore. He'll be out for a few weeks. Now, how many of you have we got tonight? Thirteen. Let's have a game. Six against seven.' As the game got underway, Ronnie chased the play barking orders. 'Go on, Jamie, push forward. That's it. Now, look up, you've got two options.' Jamie chose Bashir but his pass was less than accurate and forced him out wide. 'Wrong choice,' said Ronnie, stopping play. 'I know Bashir was in space but what about John? He was on the edge of the penalty area.'

'He was being marked,' said Jamie.

'But he wasn't completely closed down,' said Ronnie, 'and he was in a much better position.'

Jamie wasn't convinced. 'I had more chance of finding Bash.'

'Who's arguing?' said Ronnie. 'But he'd still have been way out on the left flank with defenders to beat. Get the ball to John and you could have put him through on goal. Worth a try, don't you think?'

Conor smirked at Jamie.

'Give over, will you?' said Liam.

'What?'

'Winding Jamie up.'

'I'm not.'

Jamie thought differently. The moment play resumed he was gunning for Conor. As Conor rose to meet a cross from the left, Jamie clattered him from behind.

'I'll have you, you blurt,' yelled Conor, leaping up belligerently from the turf.

'Try it,' Jamie roared back.

'Now that,' Ronnie barked, jumping between them, 'is enough.' But Liam knew it wouldn't be. Conor wasn't one to let anything ride. Never had. Never would. Sure enough, five minutes later Jamie was on the ball when Conor came storming in, studs showing. Caught on the shin, Jamie crashed to the ground. 'Are you all right, lad?' asked Ronnie anxiously. He started examining Jamie's leg.

'It's not my leg,' said Jamie. 'It's my rotten arm. I fell on it.'

'You sure?' asked Ratso.

'Of course I'm flaming sure,' cried Jamie. 'It's *my* arm, isn't it?' His face creased with pain.

'Let's take a look,' said Ronnie. He touched Jamie's wrist gently. It was enough to make Jamie cry out.

'It's starting to swell,' said Kev.

'That's it then,' said Ronnie. 'I'm taking you to the hospital.' He helped Jamie to his feet. 'I don't know,' said Ronnie. 'I ought to get a season ticket to that casualty department. They're going to wonder what I'm doing to you lads. First Gordon, now Jamie.'

Liam watched with a sinking heart as Jamie eased himself into the passenger seat. He could feel the resentment towards Conor among the squad. 'You've done it now,' he told Conor.

'Behave,' said Conor, 'it was a fair tackle.'

'Fair?' said Liam. 'You were trying to take him out and that's exactly what you've done. I'm sick of your antics, Con.'

'Get off home, lads,' said Ronnie. 'I'll be in touch before Sunday's game.' He gave Conor a long, cool look. Conor stared back, completely unfazed.

'You'd better watch yourself,' Liam whispered.

'What are you on about?'

'Just look at Ant's face. I bet you've forgotten he's Jamie's cousin.'

Conor feigned a yawn. 'I'm not scared of him.'

Ronnie must have been thinking along the same lines as Liam because he wound down his window and eyeballed Ant. 'And mark my words,' he warned, starting the engine, 'I don't want anybody taking the law into their own hands over what's happened. Got that?'

'You mean Conor gets off scot free?' Ant complained.

'I mean I'll deal with it later. Right now, I'm more bothered about Jamie's wrist. It's still swelling. Leave everything to me. Got it?'

'Got it, Ron,' came the muttered reply from the team.

'Ant?'

'Yeah yeah, I've got it.' The Diamonds shuffled away, darting hostile glances at Conor.

'Well, thanks a lot Conor,' Liam snapped as they were left alone.

'What are you having a go at me for?' asked Conor.

'You don't know, do you?' said Liam. 'Nothing gets through your thick skull. Just clear off and leave me alone.'

Conor headed for his bike then stopped. 'One thing, Liam,' he said.

'What's that?'

'You won't mention this to Mum and Dad, will you?'

'You know what?' said Liam. 'You're one selfish get.'

'But will you tell them?'

'You know I won't. I never snitch, not even on a dweeb like you.'

'Very nice,' said Conor. 'You're supposed to be my brother.'

'I know,' said Liam taking the lock off his bike. 'And right now I wish I wasn't.'

Six

Mum's out again. I don't get it. Four years and she can't have gone out more than a dozen times. Suddenly she's out two nights on the run. What gives? It even crossed my mind that she might have met somebody. Stupid really, Mum isn't like that. She isn't interested in men. It's just Cheryl putting things in my mind. But how come Mum's out again already? I tried quizzing uncle Dave but he wasn't giving anything away. That only made matters worse. The more mysteriously he acted about where she'd gone, the more annoyed I got. I decided to stay awake and wait up till she came in. I made it until one o'clock in the morning. I remember noting the time on my bedside clock. Then I must have fallen asleep. I woke up wondering what time she got in . . . or do I mean if she got in?

Seven

It was Wednesday night before Conor discovered his fate. Not that he was worried about it. Far from it, he'd completely forgotten that Ronnie would be phoning him. He had a new Nike sweatshirt and two bargain computer games, his share of the booty from Dad's trip down to the wholesalers.

'Phone call for you, Con,' shouted Mum.

'Oh, not now,' moaned Conor. 'I'm battering Liam at "Techno Warrior".'

'I don't care if you're playing "Zombie Man-Eaters from Bootle",' said Mum. 'You're answering this phone.'

'Who is it?'

'Ronnie Mintoe. Now are you coming, or not?'

'Ronnie,' Conor repeated, 'now what does he want?'

'What do you think, you div?' snorted Liam. 'It's over Jamie.' Conor gave a puzzled frown.

'Oh behave,' said Liam. 'Just how thick is your hide? That tackle.'

The dawn of understanding. 'Oh.'

'Oh is right. Now go and find out what he's got to say.' Conor might not be worried, but Liam was. He'd been worrying on Conor's behalf. He strained to hear the phone conversation. He could only make out Conor's side of it.

'Hi there Ronnie.' Pause. 'Broken it, has he?' Pause. 'That long, eh?'

A longer pause. 'You what?' Pause. 'Now hang on a minute. I didn't mean it. It was an accident.' Pause. 'Not even on the sub's bench? Oh, you've got to be kidding.' Pause. 'But . . .' Pause. 'But . . .' Then the sound of Conor replacing the receiver.

Liam met him on the landing. 'Well?'

'You're not going to believe this. I'm suspended for Sunday's game.'

'I meant Jamie. How is he?'

'He's broken his wrist. He's going to have plaster on for six weeks.'

'Poor Jamie,' said Liam.

'Poor Jamie!' exclaimed Conor. 'Poor me, more like.

All I do is tackle him and I get dropped from the team. Football *is* supposed to be a contact sport. Am I right, or am I right? It's not fair. We ought to find another side to play for.'

'So do it,' said Liam, 'I'm sticking with the Diamonds.'

'Some brother you are,' said Conor. 'I thought you'd back me up.'

'Why should I?' asked Liam. 'You're to blame for all this.'

'You mean you're taking Jamie Moore's side against me? He started it, you know.'

'Maybe,' said Liam doubtfully, 'but you had to finish it, didn't you? Who's the one who ended up in hospital?'

'Shouldn't start what you can't finish,' said Conor.

'I hope you don't mean that,' said Liam.

'Of course I mean it.'

'Then you're an even bigger divvie than I thought.'

'Who's a divvie?' asked Conor, his eyes flashing.

'You are.'

'You are, you mean.' Conor planted himself in Liam's path.

'Oh, get out of my way.'

'Make me.'

Liam tried to walk round Conor, but found his way blocked. 'This is stupid.'

'Yes, and so are you.'

'Oh, grow up Con.'

Instead of growing up, Conor shoved Liam hard against the wall. Liam reacted by throwing himself against his brother. Moments later they were struggling on the landing floor.

'What's going on?' shouted Mum from the bottom

of the stairs. 'Lenny,' she said. 'The boys are fighting again.'

'It'll blow over,' he yawned.

'Is that all you've got to say?' Mum asked tetchily.

'Knock it off, lads,' called Dad half-heartedly. But the twins carried on wrestling, Conor with his arm round Liam's neck, Liam boring his head under Conor's chin.

'I'm coming up there,' said Mum. She started running upstairs, but the fight continued. 'Oh, for goodness' sake,' Mum groaned. 'What now?'

'It was him,' Conor yelled, eager to get in the first accusation.

'No, it wasn't,' Liam shot back. 'It was him. He's the one who put a lad in hospital.'

'You said you weren't going to tell!' cried Conor, outraged. 'You promised.'

'That was before you started defending what you did,' panted Liam, still flushed from the fight.

'Now stop right there,' said Mum. 'You . . .' she was pointing to Liam, '. . . go to your room and calm down.' Liam did as he was told. 'As for you, Conor Savage, I think we need to have a little talk.'

Liam shook his head. Big deal. If Dad was included, it added up to a let-off. Conor got away with everything.

Eight

I don't believe it. She is seeing someone. It doesn't take a genius to work out where she met him. He must have chatted her up on Sunday night. They're going out again

— 31 —

this Saturday. I've tried quizzing her about him, but she's not telling. Just his name, Jack Dougan. I hate him already. I mean, what right's he got to move in on my mum? She's married to Dad, isn't she? OK, so they're separated and I've just about given up hope that they might get back together, but what's she doing seeing other men? It's way out of order. The thought of this slimy Dougan character hanging round, it makes me sick. I know, I'll tell Dad. Just wait till he finds out. He'll go mental. Nobody moves in on his lady, not unless they fancy a new face. But how can I? For starters I wouldn't know how to break it to him. Then there's the little question of us not speaking. It's all about Bashir's dad. He has a shop on the Parade next to this hooky cab firm run by Lee Ramage and Dad and they've been trying to put him out of business. Me and Dad have hardly exchanged a word since we had a row about it. So that's it. I'll just have to wait till Dad finds out for himself. It won't be long. You don't keep many secrets on an estate like the Diamond.

Then the fur's really going to fly.

Nine

It was St Valentine's Day the following Sunday, but there wasn't much love in the air in the Diamonds' changing room. They were able to field a team. Just. But no matter how much Ronnie tried to gloss over the problems there was no disguising the fact; it was a makeshift side, and an unhappy one to boot.

'I've had to do a bit of juggling with the squad,' Ronnie told the players in the changing room. 'The strike force was my main problem.'

'As in we haven't got one,' said John.

'A bit of an over-statement,' said Ronnie.

Kev wrinkled his nose. Not much.

'But you're right,' Ronnie went on. 'You'll all know by now that Jamie's out for a couple of months, and Gord will be missing a couple of games as well. What some of you might not be aware of is why Conor's absent. I've cut him from the team because of the tackle on Jamie on Monday night.' Ronnie paused for a moment, before moving on to his team selection. 'I'm putting Kev up front. He's a proven goal-scorer and he's got the natural strength to hold the ball up. Bashir, I want you to play alongside him.'

'What,' exclaimed Bashir, 'me, a striker?'

'Why not? You're quick and you've netted some good goals.'

'But what about our wing play?' asked Kev. 'We've got to have some width. You're always saying it.'

'I'm moving Liam into the left wing berth,' said Ronnie. 'It's not that much of a step from wing-back to winger, after all.' Ant glared at Liam. With Conor missing, Liam was the next best target for his anger. 'Joey, you're playing left-back. Chris, you take Kev's place in mid-field. Dougie . . .' A smile of relief from Dougie. He'd been kicking his heels on the subs' bench long enough. 'You deputise for Gordon. any questions?'

'Yes,' said Ant, pointing at Liam. 'What's he doing here?'

'Playing,' said Ronnie firmly. 'I've dropped Conor for a match to let him know I won't have breaches of discipline. But Liam's done nothing wrong, so he plays. If anyone wants to argue with that, they can walk right now. So,' he said, leaning forward to emphasize his determination to be taken seriously, 'any *sensible* questions?'

'There are a lot of us playing out of position,' said Kev. 'Are you sure this'll work?'

'No,' Ronnie replied honestly, 'I'm not, but I'm using the eleven players available to me. We're that depleted we can't even name a sub today. I suppose what I'm saying is, *you've* got to make it work.'

'Then let's stop wittering on about the game,' said Kev. 'Let's do it.' This earned the ritual battle cry, but there was no disguising its half-heartedness.

John O'Hara wasn't just speaking for himself when he gave his gloomy verdict: 'Lambs to the slaughter.'

The Diamonds took the field to the strains of *All You Need is Love* by the Beatles.

'What's that in aid of?' asked Ant.

'It's Valentine's Day,' said Ratso. 'Seemed appropriate.'

'Sure,' said Ant. 'To a moron.' He was still in a bad mood over Liam's presence.

'Well, I like it,' Ratso said stubbornly. While John Lennon was belting out of the ghetto blaster the opposition, St Bede's, were being bolstered by heckling from the Liver Bird on the way to their own match on Pitch Four.

'I hear you've got problems, McGovern,' shouted Costello.

'That's right,' said Brain Damage. 'Putting each other into hospital! What next?'

'Not many Valentines going round your team,' chuckled Tez Cronin.

'Drop dead,' snarled Kev.

'So what's it like playing without an attack?' asked Costello.

'Goal-less,' said Brain Damage. 'Or is it clue-less?'

'Ha, hardy, ha,' said a sullen Kev.

'Tell you what, Guv,' said Chris, watching the Liver Bird strutting away. 'They need a good kicking.'

'And we're the ones to give it to them,' said Ant.

'Don't take the bait,' said Kev. 'They'd love a good ruck.' The referee called the players to order. The Diamonds won the toss and played into the wind. 'We'll get the advantage in the second half,' said Kev. But it was the next few minutes which mattered. The swirling easterly wind was worth an extra player to St Bede's and they weren't slow to exploit their advantage, floating in high balls at every opportunity to test the experimental Diamonds' defence. 'Get stuck in to them,' Kev bawled at his mid-field. 'You've got to stop them getting forward.'

'Easier said than done,' panted Chris. 'They're good.'

'Not that good,' said Kev. 'We beat them last time we met.'

'You're right,' said Ratso, always ready with the match facts. 'What you didn't mention was that Conor and Jamie scored two of the goals.'

Five minutes into the game, St Bede's early possession bore fruit. Todd Welsh side-stepped a clumsy challenge by Dougie and crossed into the box. Brian Dinsdale was on hand to nod home from close range.

'Terr-ific,' groaned Kev. 'What sort of defending do you call that?' His challenge was met with sullen looks. Buoyed up by the goal, St Bede's continued to press.

First Chris, then Joey cleared their lines under pressure. 'More like it,' Kev observed from the half-way line. The Diamonds' fight-back continued when Joey brought the ball away and went on a strong run through St Bede's mid-field.

'My ball,' shouted Liam. 'Come on, Joey. Now.' Joey seemed to consider the outlet provided by Liam, then changed his mind and checked his run, finally playing it square to John. 'Why didn't you pass?' cried Liam. 'I was clear.'

Joey didn't answer. There was no need. Just before half-time the Diamonds were calling all the shots. They were defending solidly and building attacks from the back. They had one problem, the final ball.

'Hello,' called Kev. 'Remember me. I'm the front man. You're supposed to get the ball to me.'

'What do you think we're trying to do?' retorted Ratso.

'Beats me,' said Kev. 'All I know is we're not making enough clear-cut chances. What's Liam playing at? I haven't had a decent cross to go for all game.'

'That isn't Liam's fault,' said Jimmy. 'Daz and Joey are freezing him out. They're just not giving him the ball.'

'Oh aren't they?' said Kev thoughtfully. 'We'll see about that.'

But just when the Diamonds were trying to sort out their supply problem, St Bede's struck again. This time the cross came in from the left, but once more it was Brian Dinsdale who was there to finish the move. With Daz slipping at the vital moment, Dinsdale scored with a toe-poke from five yards out.

Two-nil down at the interval.

Ten

Ronnie was waiting for the boys as they trooped off the field.

'Come on, Joey,' he said. 'Speak to me.'

'What about?'

'Oh, you know very well what I mean. Why aren't you giving Liam the ball?' Joey shrugged his shoulders. 'No, you're not getting away with that,' Ronnie said, pressing him. 'What gives?' Joey was looking rather shame-face.

Not so Ant. 'I'll tell you what,' he said. 'We don't think either of the brothers should be playing. Do we lads?' Murmurs of agreement from Dougie, John, Joey and Daz.

'I thought I'd been through this once,' said Ronnie. 'It was Conor who tackled Jamie, so he's the one being punished.'

'One match?' said Ant. 'You don't call that a punishment. He'll be laughing at you.'

'Listen lad,' said Ronnie, giving Ant a hard stare. 'Team discipline's my territory. If you disagree, you know what you can do.'

'I'm with Ron,' said Kev.

Ant pulled a face. 'You would be.'

Sensing that the disagreement could get out of control, Liam took a deep breath and chipped in with his own contribution. 'I've told Conor he was wrong,' he said. 'I've been harder on him than any of you could.'

'Oh yeah, sure,' sneered Ant.

'It's true. We even had a fight.' Liam's revelation was met with sceptical looks.

'Brothers always fight,' said Ant. 'It goes with the territory.'

'I don't care if you believe me or not,' he said. 'But I'll tell you this for free. We're going the right way to getting thrashed.'

'He's right,' said Kev. 'And we can't afford to lose any more ground on the teams above us.'

'Think about it,' said Ratso, weighing in with a vital statistic. 'If we lose today and Longmoor win, we'll be eleven points adrift.'

'So you're telling us to kiss and make up?' asked Daz unimpressed.

'I'm asking you to play as a team,' said Ronnie. 'There are going to be tensions in any team, but we're cutting off our noses to spite our face.'

'Come again?' said Joey.

'He means,' Ratso explained, 'we're shooting ourselves in the foot.'

'Oh.' Joey looked a bit lost among all these noses, faces and feet.

'So are we ready to have a go?' asked Kev. 'Are we going to turn this round?' His rallying call wasn't exactly met with enthusiasm, but at least nobody had said no.

Ten minutes into the second half, things were looking up. Joey had found Liam with two passes and the Diamonds were having some success down the left.

'Keep it going,' shouted Kev. 'We've got them pinned in their own half.'

Two minutes later it was Liam who provided the Diamonds with their best chance of the match. Wrong-footing his marker with a neat drag-back he ran on into the area and fired in a blistering drive that St Bede's keeper John McDermott did well to beat out. Controlling the loose ball with his back to the goal, Bashir did brilliantly to swivel and shoot. Unfortunately, it was right down the keeper's throat and he collected it gratefully.

'Don't get frustrated,' said Kev. 'Just keep pressing and we'll get the openings.' He was proven right within seconds. John picked out Bashir with a long ball down the inside left channel. 'Bash, Bash,' called Kev. But Liam was in an even better position, storming in from the wing. Bash rolled the ball into his path and Liam drove the ball low and hard across the area where Ratso was on hand to slot the ball home. 'Right,' said Kev, 'we're back in it. Now let's keep our concentration, lads. We don't want any silly slip-ups.'

For the next ten minutes it was all Diamonds. Kev was denied twice by the lightning reflexes of John McDermott in the St Bede's goal. Liam set Bashir up with a chance to score but Bashir sliced it wide of the upright.

'They're going to crack,' said Kev. 'I can feel it.' But it was the Diamonds who cracked. Dougie was the culprit, giving away an unnecessary free kick on the edge of the area.

Daz lined up his wall. 'Left a bit, left a bit. OK, that'll do.'

Brian Dinsdale was on a hat-trick and there was no question who would take the kick. Placing the ball purposefully, he took a short run-up. As he swung his leg the Diamonds' wall jumped in time-honoured fashion. But the St Bede's striker had a few tricks up his sleeve. Instead of trying to lift his shot over the wall, he sent it scudding along the turf *under* it. Taken completely by surprise, Daz tried to get down but the ball bounced agonizingly over his outstretched palms.

Three-one to St Bede's.

'Oh, for crying out loud, Daz,' barked Ant.

'Give over,' said Liam. 'Nobody could have saved that.'

'Who asked your opinion?' snarled Ant.

Liam shook his head. Did he want to wreck the team?

'Don't let your heads go down,' shouted Kev. 'That was a fluke, completely against the run of play.'

'Trying to persuade yourself or something?' asked Brian Dinsdale, grinning broadly. Kev darted him a Medusa stare and re-started the match. In the closing minutes the Diamonds rattled the bar and post with shots from Kev and Liam.

'If there was any justice we'd be on level terms,' said Jimmy.

'At least,' said Kev. 'I just hope it isn't one of those days.' With the ref looking at his watch Liam set off on another of his runs, carving the St Bede's defence wide open. There was no time for any pretty stuff. He just booted the ball into the area. Route one paid off. Kev was on hand to head it just inside the near post. Two-three.

Kev snatched the ball and raced for the centre spot. 'We can do this,' he yelled. 'We can pull it out of the fire.'

But no sooner had he punted the ball upfield than the ref blew. They'd quite simply run out of time.

Eleven

Kev was just crossing the road by the Blue Star chippy when he heard a familiar voice.

'Hi Kev.'

He considered the teenage girl standing at the bus stop. 'Cheryl.' For a moment he hadn't even been sure it *was* his cousin.

'What's up?' she asked, smiling. 'Didn't you recognize me?'

He gave her a long, hard look. Was it the fancy black dress or the quilted jacket? She was really dressed up. She looked two or three years older than she was. 'What have you done to yourself?'

'I got blond streaks in my hair,' Cheryl replied.

Sure, that was it. The hair.

'Helen's mum did it last night,' Cheryl explained proudly. 'What do you think?'

'It's all right,' Kev grunted.

'Oh dear,' said Cheryl. 'What's the matter with you, and where are your mates?' Kev was about to answer when she cut him short. 'No,' she said, 'let me guess. It's Sunday dinner. You got beat, didn't you? Don't tell me, you needed to be alone.'

Kev dug his hands deep in his pockets. How come she could read him like a book? 'Should've won.'

'So what happened?'

Kev was about to explain when he noticed the expression on her face. 'You don't really want to know, do you?'

Cheryl shook her head. 'Not really. I'm not that

bothered about football, remember.' Kev lapsed into a brooding silence. 'Oh, go on,' said Cheryl. 'Let's have the gory details.'

Though he would never admit it, he liked telling her things. When it came to shoulders to cry on, there were none more comfortable than Cheryl's. 'The Diamonds are tearing themselves apart. Footy's all about team-work, but all the lads ever do is fight. You know the twins, Liam and Conor?'

Cheryl shook her head. 'Not really.'

'Doesn't matter, they've just joined the team. They're good, but everybody's got it in for them.'

'Why?'

'Beats me. All I know is, it's wrecking our season. The Liver Bird are watching us self-destruct and it's doing my head in.' Kev didn't need to explain who the Liver Bird were. Cheryl was no fan of Luke Costello or Brain Damage.

'The Liver Bird?' she said. 'Ugh, they give me the creeps.'

'They should,' said Kev. 'They're the devil team. I'd love to wipe the smile off their faces.'

'I hope you do,' said Cheryl. 'They're obnoxious.'

'Anyway,' said Kev. 'What are you all dolled up for?'

Cheryl pulled a face. 'Promise you're not going to make fun of me.'

'What?'

'Go on, promise.' She searched her mind for a good oath. 'By the sacred turf of Goodison Park.'

'OK, I promise, I won't skit you.'

'I'm going to the pictures.'

'What, with Helen?'

'Yes, but not just Helen.'

'Who then?'

'Forgotten what day it is?' asked Cheryl.

Kev remembered Ratso's tune at the match. 'It's St Valentine's . . . You mean you've got a date?'

Cheryl blushed. 'Not a date. Just that new Meg Ryan film, then a McDonald's. Not what you'd call a date.'

'Who are you going with?'

Cheryl tugged at her hair nervously. 'It's a foursome. Helen and Mike Rathbone. Me and Mark Westry.'

'What, the one in Year Nine?' Cheryl nodded. 'And aunty Pat and uncle Dave are letting you?'

'They think it's nice. The only rule is, I've got to be in by five.'

Kev didn't know what to make of it. He did feel a slight twinge of jealousy. Cheryl's mate Helen had always had a crush on him. It was only a *slight* twinge however. Girls hadn't landed on Planet McGovern yet. 'First Mum, then you,' he said. 'Must be something in the water.'

'How do you mean?'

'Oh nothing, just that Mum is seeing somebody. You were right, she did cop off.'

'So I heard,' said Cheryl.

'Did aunty Pat tell you?'

'Of course.'

'What did she say? What's he like?'

'Nice.'

'Is that all you've got to say?'

'What am I supposed to say? She deserves to meet somebody who treats her properly.'

'What about Dad?'

'What about him?' Cheryl snorted. Neither she nor aunty Pat and uncle Dave had any time for Tony McGovern. 'He's been rotten to aunty Carol. She doesn't owe him anything.'

'He's still my dad.'

Cheryl nodded. 'I know,' she said quietly.

'Uh oh,' said Kev, spotting Mark Westry hovering on the opposite side of the road. Helen and Mike Rathbone were getting off the bus further down the road. 'I'd better be off. Here's lover boy.'

Cheryl chuckled. 'See you soon, Kev. Good luck with the Diamonds.'

'Thanks.' But it wasn't just the Diamonds Kev needed luck with. All the way home he'd been thinking about Mr Nice, so when he saw the flowers on the kitchen table he almost flipped. It was a bouquet, still in its fancy wrapper. Twelve red roses. For a moment, Kev tried to convince himself they were from Dad. Stupid idea. Flowers weren't his style. He didn't know a hollyhock from a hydrangea. Feelings weren't his style either, unless it was the numbness you get when the boot goes in. Checking Mum wasn't around, Kev read the card: *To my valentine. Love Jack.*

PART TWO

Backs to the Wall

*It has been an up and down season.
Sometimes we play well, sometimes we
don't. We will get it right though.*

Paul Ince of Liverpool and
England

One

Liam threw the control pad to the floor. 'This is stupid,' he said. 'I've got better things to do.'

'Oh, come on,' sniggered Conor. 'What could be better than getting tanked by your younger, better brother at "Teen Raider"?'

Liam looked out at the driving rain. It was laced with sleet and sparkled in the dying light of a chilly Tuesday evening. 'Just about anything,' he said.

'Another game?' suggested Conor.

'No.'

'I'll let you ride the hover-bike.'

'No.'

'I'll let you get to the Power Platform before I give chase.'

'For crying out loud, Conor, no. Get Dad to play.' Then, with venom: 'He's more your own age.'

'What's with you?' asked Conor. 'You usually take defeat more gracefully than this.' A mischievous grin. 'You've had plenty of practice.'

'I shouldn't be talking to you,' said Liam, 'never mind play the Gamestation with you.'

'Oh, not this Diamonds thing again.'

'Yes,' said Liam, 'The Diamonds. You could have turned up last night for training. Typical of you, create the problem then leave me to take the flak.'

'There's an easy way out,' said Conor.

'I am *not* quitting the Diamonds,' Liam told him forcefully. It wasn't the first time they'd had this conversation.

Conor shook his head. 'Don't see why not.'

'It's called loyalty,' said Liam.

'What about loyalty to me? They booted me out, the mings.'

'They did not boot you out,' cried Liam. 'You were suspended for one game. *One game*. For half-crippling somebody. Get real, Ronnie bent over backwards to go easy on you.'

'Oh yeah, as if.'

Liam could feel the frustration growing. Why did he let Conor get him going like this? 'He did,' Liam insisted. 'You broke Jamie's wrist. What do you expect?'

'I didn't break his wrist. He fell funny.'

Liam wasn't in the mood for another game of Did/Didn't. One of them had to act his age. 'Whatever.' He gave Conor a sideways glance. 'Con?'

'Yes.'

'You *are* going to return to the Diamonds, aren't you?'

Conor flopped onto his bed and tucked his hands behind his head. 'Dunno.'

'We need you. It's Orrell Park Rangers on Sunday. They battered us last time.'

'Nice to feel wanted,' said Conor, a smile playing on his lips. 'But it'll take more than a bit of creeping from you to get me back.'

'OK,' said Liam, 'give. What are you after?'

Conor stared up at the ceiling. 'You could always get Ant to do a bit of grovelling.'

Liam took a deep breath. That's right. Ask for the impossible. 'Oh sure,' he said. 'That's really going to happen, isn't it?'

'It better had,' said Conor. 'Because you're in deep doo-doo without me.'

Liam's eyes narrowed. Conor was right. Without either of their natural strikers, the Diamonds were going to struggle. 'You're enjoying this, aren't you, you creep?'

That's when Dad poked his head round the door. 'Not arguing again, are you lads?'

'Would we, Dad?' asked Conor cheerfully.

'Of course not,' said Dad, stringing out the joke. 'Never a cross word between my boys.'

Liam took advantage of the interruption to bail out. 'I'm getting out of here,' he snorted irritably. He plodded miserably downstairs and dropped into a chair in front of the TV.

'Something up?' asked Mum.

'Conor.'

'What's he done now?'

'He won't play for the Diamonds.'

'I'm sure that's not true.'

'It is. He just told me.'

Mum smiled. 'He's winding you up. He loves his football.'

'Not as much as he likes being a pain.'

'Why don't you get your dad to have a word with him?'

'He's up there right now.'

'There you are then,' said Mum. 'The perfect opportunity.'

Liam tried to picture Dad having a word with Conor. The idea didn't exactly fill him with confidence. 'Maybe.'

'No maybe about it,' said Mum. 'You get up those stairs and sort it out.'

Liam gave a resigned nod and made his way upstairs. 'Dad,' he called from outside Conor's room. He didn't answer. He and Conor were making too much noise over the computer game.

'Oh Dad, you rat,' yelled Conor. 'You got the sky buggy.'

'Just watch me go,' said Dad. 'Eat my dust, sucker.' There was more laughter as the pair pounded the control pads.

'Dad,' said Liam, raising his voice.

'What's that Liam? Oh no, laser attack, laser attaa-aaack!'

'Talk to Dad?' Liam thought. 'What's the point? It'd be like talking to Conor all over again.' With that he went into his room and slammed the door.

Two

Later that same evening Kev came to a decision. 'Mum,' he said, approaching her as she loaded the washing machine.

'Yes?'

'Can I phone Dad?' Mum stiffened. Kev gave her a long look. No, he thought, you don't want me mentioning Jack Dougan and his lousy roses, do you? 'Can I?'

'You can try,' said Mum finally. 'But don't be disappointed if he isn't in.'

'I've got the number of his mobile,' said Kev. 'He gave it to me the last time we went out.' He omitted to add *and the last time we had a row*.

'Three guesses why he needs a mobile,' said Mum, tension lines forming round the corners of her mouth.

'I know what he is,' Kev murmured, remembering all the times he'd seen him driving Lee Ramage around the estate in his flashy BMW. 'You don't need to keep reminding me.'

'Go on then,' said Mum, softening. 'He is your dad.'

'Yes,' said Kev. 'He is.' *And not Jack Dougan.* Mum hated Kev contacting Dad. She'd made a lot of mistakes in her life and every one of them was called Tony McGovern. Kev tapped out the number regardless. 'Dad?' There was a pause at the other end, then a familiar man's voice.

'Well well, now this is a turn up for the book,' said Dad. 'I thought you weren't talking to me.' Kev remembered the exchange about Dad and Lee Ramage's dirty tricks campaign against Mr Gulaid's shop.

'Funny,' said Kev, 'I thought it was the other way round.'

'Yes well,' said Dad drily. 'It takes two to tango, I suppose. What's the matter?'

'I want to see you,' said Kev. He lowered his voice. 'I've got something to tell you.'

'So tell me.'

'Not on the phone,' said Kev. 'I don't want Mum to hear.'

'Got you,' said Dad. 'Sensitive matter, is it?' Kev didn't like Dad's tone. He was making fun of him. 'So can we meet?'

'Sure, I'll take you and Gareth out.'

'Why's Gareth got to come?'

'Your mum will think it's funny if he doesn't.'

Kev considered this for a moment. 'OK, when?'

'Can't manage tomorrow – business. Thursday, Friday. Tell you what, I'll take you bowling next Monday. Can't do it any earlier.'

Kev tutted. Monday! Didn't Dad know . . .?

'No Kev,' said Dad, 'I haven't forgotten, you've got training. I'll pick Gareth up from your mum's and you from South Road on my way back.'

Kev was relieved that Dad had remembered the Diamonds, but he had one problem. 'Gareth can't bowl.'

'He can have a go,' said Dad. 'They have these gizmos for the little kids. Helps them roll the ball. Besides, he'll be happy stuffing his face.'

'Right, next Monday it is.'

'See you son.'

'See you Dad.'

Mum was rummaging in the cupboard. 'Funny,' she said. 'I thought I bought another conditioner.' She was throwing cartons and bottles about. Her way of letting off steam. Kev phoning Dad had put her on edge. It always did. 'Well,' she said, 'can His Lordship manage a few minutes of his valuable time?'

'He's taking us out next Monday,' said Kev. 'That OK?'

'Yes, it's fine. What are you doing?'

'He's taking us bowling.'

'You'll enjoy that.' Her voice sounded flat.

'Can I watch the footy on the TV?' asked Kev.

'What is it?'

'FA Cup replay.'

'Everton, is it?' Kev tutted. He'd been going on about little else for three days. 'Well,' said Mum. 'I don't know much about football.'

'I know,' said Kev. 'It shows.' As he walked into the living room he was feeling really angry at Mum. How could she carry on as if nothing had happened? What about the roses? What about the slimeball who gave them to her? Gareth was watching cartoons. His giggling annoyed Kev nearly as much as the roses. Snatching the remote control off Gareth, Kev changed channels.

'Mum,' bawled Gareth. 'Kev's turned the telly over and I was watching cartoons.'

'Oh, pipe down,' said Kev. 'It's your bedtime in ten minutes. You've been watching them for ages. Besides, they're all repeats. The mouse ties the cat's tail to the car bumper and waves him on his way.'

Gareth wasn't placated. '*Mum*!'

'What now?' asked Mum as she staggered into the living room with a pile of ironing.

'He turned the telly over,' said Gareth, turning an accusing glare at Kev. 'He never even asked.'

'He's had his telly,' said Kev.

'Let him have ten minutes,' said Mum. 'He'll be up in bed after that and you can watch what you want.'

'You always side with him,' Kev sulked. 'I'm going upstairs till he's out of the way. I hate him.'

'You can't hate your brother,' said Mum.

'Just watch me.'

Once upstairs Kev started regretting his short temper. He was missing the build-up and he didn't even know the team selection yet. It would be just like Mum to give Gareth extra time up to spite him. Then he'd miss some of the first half. He was trying to work out how to back down without losing too much face when he heard a car pull up. He glanced into the street. Through the drumming rain he could make out a tall man in a full-length navy blue coat alarming his car. A black Mondeo. Brand new.

'Nice,' said Kev. He was about to move away from

the window when he saw the man walking towards the front door. The doorbell rang.

'What the . . . ?'

'Sorry to call so late,' came a man's voice. 'But I was passing. It's on my way. Are we on for Saturday?'

Mum's voice was harder to make out. She was deliberately keeping it low. Straining to hear, Kev caught a few snatches of conversation: '. . . after a baby-sitter,' '. . . letting the kids know,' '. . . you know I do.'

Feigning nonchalance, he jogged downstairs. 'Who's at the door?' he asked, peering over Mum's shoulder.

'Oh,' Mum said, her voice betraying more than a hint of guilt. 'This is Jack. Jack, my son Kevin.'

Kev inspected the man standing at the door. He was tall, very blond with vivid blue eyes. Then there were his cheekbones. What did they call that look? Yes, chiselled. He looked like a member of one of those boys bands, but about ten years older, and harder.

'Hello,' said Kev guardedly.

'Hello there, Kev,' said Jack. He offered his hand, but Kev just stared at it. It was as big as a shovel.

Mum was nervous, hovering uncertainly between them. She made a decision. 'You may as well come in for a coffee,' she said. 'Seeing as you're here.'

'Just half a cup,' said Jack. 'I've got a meeting in town.' Kev glanced at his watch. Five to eight. Bit late for a meeting.

Mum led the way into the kitchen. She was still jittery. 'Aren't you watching the match, Kev?' she asked.

Kev was reluctant to move. He was curious about the new man in Mum's life.

'It's not on yet,' he told her. 'Just Andy Gray droning on.'

'Go easy,' said Jack. 'He was a good servant for the club.'

'Are you an Evertonian?' asked Kev.

'True Blue,' said Jack.

'So how come you aren't watching the match?'

'It's the job,' said Jack. 'Funny hours.'

Kev was intrigued. 'Why, what do you do?'

An anguished look from Mum. Kev had half-guessed before Jack answered. 'I'm a copper.'

Kev gave a low whistle. He had something to tell Dad all right!

Three

Liam sat in his usual window-seat, perching uneasily on the broad sill listening to the church bells. Next to him was a half-eaten bowl of Weetabix, the wrappers from two Nutri-grain bars and a book of Viking Myths.

'Liam.' Conor. Let him stew. '*Li-am.*' Liam continued to blot out Conor's insistent voice. He liked listening to the church bells. Not that he ever went. It was a peaceful sound, that's all. 'LIAM!!' Unlike his stupid brother.

'What?'

'Are you having a game?'

Liam picked up his book. 'I'm reading.'

Conor wrinkled his nose in distaste. 'Boring.'

'OK,' said Liam, caving in as usual. 'What are we playing?'

'"Tunnel Rats".'

Liam laid the book face down on the sill. 'Yes, all right. On one condition.'

'Name it.'

'You don't bottle out of the match. You are coming?'

'I said I was.'

'And no messing about. We get there on time?'

'I told you, didn't I?' said Conor. 'I'll be there to give you losers a helping hand.'

Liam snorted. Typical of Conor. When it came to the Diamonds, it was always *you*, never *us*. Conor considered himself a big fish in a small pool.

'Don't put yourself out,' said Liam.

Conor grinned. 'You know me, our kid, I never do.'

Liam resisted the temptation to snap back. 'Let's play the game.' It was a familiar pattern. Conor intent on his game, quick off the blocks and right into his stride. Liam trying to look indifferent, but dying to win for once.

'Watch this,' said Conor, jumping and turning at the same time, a move that sent his tunnel sled riding up on the roof of the tunnel. 'Yiss! Never fails.'

Liam had tried the move, but he always turned his sled over. Instead, he pursued a straight line.

'Don't know why you're doing that,' said Conor, glancing at the bottom half of the split screen. 'You'll lose time over the floor grids.'

'I know that!' snapped Liam.

'So why not take the same line as me?'

'You know very well why not,' Liam retorted with a scowl. 'Because I can't do it.'

'You know what they say, pupil of mine,' Conor gloated. 'Practice makes perfect.' Liam chewed his lip and followed Conor home. 'Beat you by fifty seconds,' said Conor. 'Ready for level two?'

'Not if we plan to make it to Jacob's Lane on time,' said Liam.

'We'll make it.'

'Conor, you promised.'

'OK, OK,' said Conor, 'don't get your knickers in a twist.'

The only thing that'll untwist my knickers, thought Liam, is you learning to grow up.

'Sub!' Conor exclaimed in dismay. 'Stinking rotten sub!'

'That's right,' said Ronnie. 'You're sub.' The Diamonds looked on, enjoying Conor's discomfort.

'So who's your attack?'

'Same as last week,' said Ronnie. 'Kevin and Bashir.'

'A mid-fielder and a winger? Some team selection that is!'

'Maybe,' Ronnie bristled, 'but it's my selection. And as far as I know, I am still manager of the Diamonds.' Conor shrugged his shoulders.

'What do you think you're doing?' Liam demanded, pulling Conor aside as the Diamonds clattered out into the corridor.

'Just pointing out that Ronnie's off his head, that's all.'

'Oh behave,' said Liam. 'If you'd bothered to turn up on Monday, you'd have been an automatic choice.' Ant was eavesdropping from the changing room doorway.

'Butt out, you,' said Conor. 'I'm talking to my brother.'

'I'll tell you this, lad,' Ant said, 'you're not fit to wear the shirt. I don't care what Ronnie says, you don't deserve to be on the bench, never mind in the team.'

'Yes,' Liam replied, 'well, like Ronnie says, he chooses the team.' Ant turned away, shaking his head.

'Honestly,' said Liam. 'Why can't you just keep your mouth shut and let the dust settle?'

'Why should I?' asked Conor. 'Meffs like him aren't fit to kiss my boots.'

Five minutes into the match Conor's reservations about the team selection were beginning to look justified. The Diamonds were looking jaded and toothless in attack. Their mid-field play lacked bite and their forward moves were breaking down in confusion.

'Get a grip, lads,' shouted Kev. 'Start working for each other.' But it was Orrell Park who were working for each other. They were doing all the pressing and were only denied the opening goal by a low save from Daz at the foot of the post. 'We need to ring the changes,' Kev muttered to Bashir. 'There's no shape to our play. I feel like a spare part up here. I'm no striker.'

Bashir nodded. 'That goes for me too.'

They both gave Ronnie a hopeful look, but Ronnie ignored them. 'More direct,' the manager shouted. 'Get it through to the front men.' John and Ratso did their best to work the ball through but an intervention by Orrell Park put the Diamonds under pressure again.

'This is a shambles,' said Kev. Within thirty seconds it was more than a shambles. It was a disaster. Dougie missed a speculative ball into the box and Orrell Park flicked it goalward from close range. 'Not again!' groaned Kev.

But it was true. They were one-nil down.

'John, Ratso,' Kev shouted. 'You've got to make things happen. And you, Liam, there's no link play. We might as well be sitting here on deck chairs for all the service we're getting.' Liam hung his head. They weren't the only ones who were being left in the cold. It was back to the old routine for him too. Joey wasn't giving him even a sniff of the ball. To make matters worse, Conor wasn't helping. He was grinning, actually smiling that the Diamonds were trailing. It wasn't lost on Ronnie. He was giving Conor daggers.

Two minutes before half-time it got even worse for the Diamonds. Ant slipped midway inside his own half and Orrell Park took advantage to drive forward and go two-nil up.

'Pathetic,' stormed Kev. 'Absolutely pathetic.' He meant the team performance, but Liam could have said the same about Conor's antics. With a brother like him, who needed enemies?

Four

The half-time talk began with a confession.

'This'll be short,' said Ronnie. 'I'll hold my hands up, lads. I got it wrong.'

Ant gave Conor a long, hard look. 'You don't mean you're bringing him on?' There was hatred in his voice.

'Yes, Anthony, I mean exactly that. I've tried the combination of Kevin and Bashir up front and it hasn't worked. Kev, I want you back in mid-field. We're a car without an engine. We've got to start competing.' A look of relief crossed Kev's face. 'Conor, you'll partner Bashir in attack. Dougie, you're off I'm afraid.'

'Look at Conor,' Ant whispered in disgust. 'Talk about the cat who's swallowed the cream.'

'What was that?' asked Ronnie.

'Nothing Ron, nothing at all.'

'It had better be nothing,' Ronnie warned. 'Now listen up, lads. Bringing Conor on will do no good at all if we keep playing the way we are. Here's how we line up. Jimmy, Chris, Ant and Joey will make up the back four. John, Peter, Kevin and Liam, you're the midfield. Bashir and Conor are playing up front. Liam and Jimmy, your brief is to get wide. And that, Joey, means Liam's got to get his share of the ball.' Joey lowered his eyes. 'That's right,' said Ronnie. 'I have noticed you leaving him out. I thought we'd got over that little problem against St Bede's.'

'Sorry Ron,' said Joey.

Ant and Daz darted him glances, as if to ask: *What are you saying sorry for?*

'Now scrap for the ball,' said Ronnie, 'and move it forward with a bit of pace. You've got to turn that defence. If we come away from this game with any less than a draw you can say goodbye to any hopes of the championship. Now, has anybody got anything to say?'

'I have,' said Liam. Eyes turned his way. With the exception of Jimmy, Kev, and Bashir, they were universally hostile, and that included Conor.

'Go on, son.'

'We're all Diamonds,' said Liam. 'Can't we just bury our differences and play for each other?' He looked round hopefully. He may as well have asked everybody to dress as Girl Guides.

'Well said,' Ronnie told Liam as the players drifted back onto the pitch.

'Thanks,' said Liam, 'but I don't think they took much notice.'

'Too right,' said Conor, catching up with Liam.

'Bury our differences,' he said, mimicking Liam. 'You big wimp. How soppy can you get?'

'You could have helped,' said Liam.

'How's that?'

'That apology I keep mentioning.'

'You can whistle,' said Conor. 'I'm not apologizing to anyone.' To avoid any further argument, Liam hurried away.

'Let it go,' Kev said encouragingly, 'you did your best. Your Conor's as stubborn as Joey, Daz and Ant. We've just got to play through it.'

'And you reckon they'll forget it?'

'Possibly.'

'Then you don't know our Conor.'

As play resumed Kev's presence in mid-field started to make a difference. After a series of his usual biting tackles, his fellow mid-fielders began to take heart. Orrell Park were being forced steadily back.

'Come on, lads,' shouted Kev. 'We can get back into this.' As if to prove his words, Liam collected the ball from a reluctant Joey Bannen and raced forward, releasing Bashir. Bashir took it to the goal-line and whipped it across the goal-mouth. Orrell Park were grateful to put it behind for a corner.

'I'll take it,' said Liam. Spotting Conor on the far post, he flighted it towards him.

'My ball!' roared Conor. The ball flicked off his forehead into the net. Two-one. 'And that,' Conor boasted triumphantly, 'is my goal.'

'Big-headed beggar,' observed Ant sourly.

Kev ran his hands through his hair. The Diamonds weren't out of jail yet. 'Come on, lads,' he urged. 'That should get us moving.'

It didn't. Joey might not be ignoring Liam quite as

blatantly but there was no crispness or flow to the Diamonds' play. The game was developing into a scrappy war of attrition. The one bit of good news in the ten minutes following the goal came from the touch-line.

'Guv,' shouted the substituted Dougie Long. 'News from Pitch Two. Longmoor are losing.'

'Who to?'

'It's Ajax Aintree,' Ratso informed him. 'Top of the table clash.'

'Hear that?' Kev shouted. 'Longmoor are losing. So let's go for it.'

Again it was Liam who responded. This time he took the ball from Joey, almost wrestling it from him. Taking on his marker he cut infield onto his left foot and drove it nearside to Bashir. Bashir flicked it invitingly back into his path.

'Hit it,' yelled Kev. Liam didn't need a written invitation. Setting himself, he lashed the ball in.

'Goal!' shrieked Ratso. 'Absolute peach.' Liam blinked disbelievingly for a second then raced off down the touch-line, arms raised in celebration. Kev and Bashir pursued him. Nobody else did.

'Two-all,' Kev reminded his players. 'Let's go for that winner.'

Kev, Bashir and Liam did just that, driving forward, swopping passes, playing for each other. It couldn't be said for the rest of the team. Most of them were merely going through the motions. As for Conor, he seemed content to swagger round, basking in the glory of his headed goal.

'Oh, wake up Diamonds,' cried Kev as they gave the ball away on the right. 'It's like you don't want to win.'

And win they didn't. Kev skied a chance from five

yards out and Liam hit the bar from an acute angle.
Two-all at full time.

Five

I've had a rotten Sunday.

*For starters, we squandered the chance to climb the table.
Our draw didn't sound too bad until I heard the other
results. Sure, Longmoor lost, but it was to Ajax. They're the
new leaders, and they're ten whole points ahead of us. With
just seven games to go it'll take a miracle to catch them. But
the really bad news came from Liver Bird's game. They
won again and that means they've leap-frogged Longmoor
into second place. Just look at this for a table:*

	Pl	W	D	L	Pts
Ajax Aintree	15	10	4	1	34
Liver Bird	15	10	3	2	33
Longmoor Celtic	15	9	4	2	31
Northend United	15	8	4	3	28
St Patrick's Thistle	15	7	4	4	25
Rough Diamonds	15	7	3	5	24

*Look at it, I mean look at it. The Liver Bird, as in Costello
and Brain Damage, my two worst enemies, a point off the
top. They're not even that bothered about football. Aggro's
their game. They only joined the league to spite us. And here
they are, second! It's criminal, an absolute nightmare. If
they took the title it'd be the end. I mean it, the end.*

*So I came away from Jacob's Lane completely gutted. All
the way home I was kicking cans and booting fences. Then*

*what do I find when I get home? Only that this Jack feller
had invited himself round for Sunday dinner.*

 *What's more, Mum was glowing. Like she had this light
inside her. She was fussing over him like he was royalty or
something, not some sneaky copper. She laughed at all his
jokes, this girly laugh. I was embarrassed for her. She's even
stopped smoking for him. That's right,* for him. *Years me
and Gareth have been trying to get her to give up, then he's
on the scene for a couple of weeks and she does it, just like
that. All the time Dougan was there the same thought kept
on running through my head. What was Dad going to
make of it? Part of me pretended it didn't matter. Dad had
made his choice all those years ago, walking out on us. So
what right would he have complaining now? But there was
another part of me. The part that's Tony McGovern to the
core. And you know what that bit was saying?* Leave her
alone, Dougan. She doesn't belong with you. She
belongs with Dad. *But convincing Mum of that isn't
going to be easy. She really thinks this copper is something
special.*

Six

While Kev was eyeballing Jack Dougan over Sunday
lunch, Liam and Conor were on the point of declaring
World War Three. Liam was the first back home.

 'Good match?' asked Mum, rinsing a paintbrush in
turps. She'd been glossing the back door. Liam flung
his kit into the laundry basket and stomped into the
living room where he sat simmering. Dad put his copy
of *Men's Health* down and gave him an amused look.

Mum was more concerned. 'Liam?' she asked. 'Is everything all right?'

'Ask him,' said Liam, pointing at Conor as he wheeled his bike past the front window.

'Oh, you can't have been fighting again!'

'Why not?' asked Dad. 'That's what brothers are for. Me and our Joe and George did nothing but, and we turned out OK.'

'You call this OK?' asked Mum. 'You said you'd sort this chaos while I painted that door.' She indicated the pile of stock. A week before it had covered half the living room floor. Now it occupied two-thirds and was advancing every day.

'Oh, it slipped my mind,' groaned Dad. 'I told you Karen, I'll have it shifted in the morning.'

'You'd better,' Mum fumed. 'Or I'm chucking it in the back yard. And what about your weights? I nearly broke my neck on them this morning?'

'I'll move them too.'

'You'd better.' Having fired a ritual salvo at Dad, she turned back to Liam. 'So what are you squabbling about this time?'

'He spoils everything.'

Conor appeared in the doorway. 'Is he talking about me?' he asked.

'Do you know anybody else round here who lets his mates down?'

'What do you mean by that?'

'You, of course,' said Liam, glaring at the TV.

Conor planted himself in front of the screen. 'Go on,' he said. 'I want to hear this.'

Liam stood up and met Conor's eyes with an icy stare. 'Are you trying to tell me you don't know what I'm on about?'

'That's right. I scored, didn't I?'

'Yes,' Liam replied, 'and you did that for yourself.'

Conor looked at Dad. 'Hear that? Didn't I tell you he talks rubbish?' Dad smiled, then seeing Liam and Mum glaring at him, he went po-faced.

'Rubbish, eh?' roared Liam. 'For starters, I gave you plenty of opportunity to apologize. What do you think that little speech was for? But would you take the hint? Oh no, not Conor High-and-Mighty Savage.'

'You could have told me,' said Conor.

Liam threw up his arms in exasperation. 'I shouldn't need to. That's the sort of thing you do off your own bat.'

'So what else am I supposed to have done wrong?'

'Just about everything,' Liam told him.

Mum and Dad were listening to the exchange without interrupting. Dad, as usual, had decided to let it blow itself out. Besides, he'd started doing a few barbell curls. Mum was getting agitated.

'See,' said Conor. 'He can't think of anything else.'

'Oh no? How's about nearly having a fight with Ant. And grinning your stupid head off every time something went wrong . . .' Conor turned away. '. . . *And*,' Liam shouted at his back, 'playing like a complete divvy.' He started prancing around, giving his best divvy impression. 'Look at me, I'm Conor Savage. I'm far too important to play with this lot. I'm just going to stand here and score the sitters.'

'It wasn't a sitter,' Conor yelled. 'It was a cracking goal.'

'It was about the only thing you did.'

Mum's patience finally snapped. This storm wasn't even beginning to blow itself out. 'Enough!' she cried, clapping her hands. 'That's enough.'

'Oh, I don't know,' said Dad, flopping onto the carpet to do his abdominal crunches. 'I was starting to enjoy it.'

'Oh, do shut up,' said Mum. 'You aren't helping with your stupid wisecracks. Don't you take anything seriously?'

'Cor, sorry for breathing.'

'Now,' said Mum in her best I-Could've-Been-a-Teacher voice, 'I want you to get up those stairs this minute. Conor, you're going to put those dirty football kits in the wash . . .'

'I'll put my own in,' Conor interrupted. 'I'm not touching his.' He glared at Liam's kit as if it was impregnated with cholera.

'You'll do exactly as you're told,' said Mum. 'Liam, you're having first shower.'

Liam marched angrily into the hall, but Conor caught up with him at the bottom of the stairs. 'Put your own rotten kit away,' he said.

'Mum told you to do it,' said Liam. He wasn't too excited about Conor touching his kit, but the way he felt he was determined to say anything that would annoy his brother.

'Well, I'm not doing it,' said Conor. 'So you put the things away and *I'll* get the first shower.'

He tried to push past, but Liam wasn't about to back down. 'Oh no you don't,' he said.

'Get out of my way.'

'Make me.'

And that was it. Conor flashed out a clenched fist that narrowly missed Liam's right ear. Liam tried to retaliate but toppled backwards, cracking his cheek on the wall. His whole face went numb. Try as he might, Liam couldn't stop the tears spilling down his cheeks.

'I don't believe it!' cried Mum, rushing out of the living room. 'Two seconds and you're at it again. 'Lenny!'

Dad had lost the superior smile. Even he was losing patience now. Scrambling to his feet, he grabbed the pair of them by the scruff of the neck, and he marched them upstairs. 'You,' he said to Conor, 'in there. And you,' to Liam. 'In there.'

'But I've banged my face,' Liam protested. 'It hurts like mad.'

'Oh, belt up Liam,' said Dad, 'you're such a rotten wimp.' Having half-pushed, half-thrown the twins into their rooms he bawled at them from the landing. 'And don't you dare come out until you've cooled down.'

Liam listened to Dad's footfalls on the stairs. The sound was almost drowned out by the frantic beating of his heart. And all the time he sat nursing his sore cheek and his equally bruised pride, Dad's words kept coming back.

Wimp, wimp, wimp.

Seven

The following Monday evening saw the Diamonds trying to learn the lessons of their disappointing two-all draw.

'Cross it, cross it,' Ronnie shouted breathlessly. The training session had turned out to be a revelation. It was Liam. Nobody had expected him to play with such skill and strength. Twice he had sped down the threadbare, criminally uneven pitch at South Road with a turn of speed that left everybody trailing in his wake. Except Bashir of course, but even the Diamonds' quickest player was pushed to keep up. Liam was on fire.

Wimp, am I? 'Want a cross, do you?' barked Liam, striking the ball with such ferocity that it cannoned against the upright, flattening Ratso on the rebound.

'Can you do that again?' asked Ronnie.

'Anytime,' said Liam. *I'll show you, Dad.* His eyes were like black diamonds, hard and flashing with anger.

'What's he on, Guv?' asked Jimmy admiringly, 'three Shredded Wheat?'

'Beats me,' said Kev. 'But we could do with a few months' supply for the whole team. He's lethal tonight.' Conor listened sullenly. Did they have to praise his dipstick of a brother?

'Go on then, Liam,' said Ronnie, seeing a little light at the end of a long, dark tunnel. 'Show us what you can do.' Ant and Joey were also showing an interest. They were plotting to show Liam a time-honoured defensive ploy of their own – the sandwich.

'Fine by me,' said Liam, gritting his teeth. His mind was a vulture, picking over the carcass of the last 24 hours. Two fights with Conor, followed by an enforced truce. Dad calling him a wimp like that and refusing to apologize even when Mum discovered a bump the size of an egg on his temple. Suddenly, Liam hated everyone. Ant, Joey and Daz for giving him stick. Conor for being . . . well, Conor. Dad for siding with Conor and Mum for being even-handed about everything even when he was the angel of all-justice and Conor was so obviously the demon of total scumminess.

'Then do it.' said Ant, unimpressed.

The tone of his voice stung Liam into action. Dribbling the ball under close control he advanced on Ant and Joey in defence. *Want some, do you?* he thought as they closed menacingly.

'He's got some pace, that lad,' said Ronnie admiringly.

'Yes, but he'll need more than pace if he's going to get past those two,' said Kev. He could read their minds and what he saw was the stuff of nightmares.

Liam glimpsed a space between Ant and Joey. Joey had been slightly quicker off the blocks and left himself exposed. As Joey challenged him Liam thrust out an arm, catching him across the throat.

'Accidental,' said Kev, covering for Liam.

'Oh sure,' said Ronnie. 'The old accidentally-on-purpose. Still,' he added with a smile, 'it's what you can get away with, isn't it?' Seeing Joey go down Ant lunged in only to discover his man had hurdled his oustretched leg and lost him.

'Foul play,' gurgled Joey, still smarting from the hand-off.

'Play on,' said Ronnie, impressed by Liam's determination. 'Legitimate self-defence.' Liam shrugged off a fierce challenge by Chris and lobbed the oncoming Daz. Conor was left with the simplest of tap-ins.

'Predator!' he roared, raising his arms in a victory salute. Only nobody was paying any attention. Liam was the star turn.

'Come over,' shouted Ronnie. 'Take the weight off your feet.' The boys flopped on the grass around him. 'There are a few bits of good news tonight,' he said. 'For a start, I'd like to welcome Gord back.' Gord smiled. 'Though Gord has told me he's been cleared to play, I'm not willing to risk that shoulder in a full game quite yet. You're sub, son.' Gord nodded. 'Second, I can tell you that Jamie's on the mend. It looks like he'll have the plaster off in two or three weeks.' Ant gave Conor a steely glare. Conor looked right through him. 'Finally, I've got the draw for the Challenge Cup quarter final. You're not going to believe this.'

'Not Longmoor.'

'More interesting than that.'

'Ajax?'

'Closer to home.'

'You're kidding!' exclaimed Kev, catching on.

'What's he on about?' asked Chris.

'It's the Liver Bird, isn't it?' asked Kev. 'We've drawn the flaming Liver Bird.'

'Give that man a banana,' said Ronnie. 'I thought you'd appreciate it.'

'This one we've got to win,' said Kev.

'Dead right,' said Chris. 'We're not going to let the scum get one over on us.' But no one else responded Kev couldn't believe it. A few weeks ago the Diamonds would have ripped the head of anybody who so much as looked at them the wrong way. Now the Savage brothers and their enemies were too busy with their own strychnine-laced rivalry to get excited about the draw.

'So when's it played?' asked Dougie.

'A week on Sunday,' said Ratso. 'St Patrick's Thistle in the league then the War of the Diamond. It's our Derby match.'

'Grudge match, more like,' said Kev, savouring the prospect. He was happy. He loved a good battle. He just couldn't understand how the others could be so offhand. Where was their pride, their passion? He was beginning to have real doubts about their appetite for the contest. If he'd seen the exchange of looks between Daz, Joey and Liam, Conor and Ant, and even between Liam and Conor he would have been more worried. They had their own ideas about a grudge match.

'I think there's someone here for you,' said Ronnie, nodding to Kev. His expression said it all. Ronnie Mintoe had no time for the Diamonds' scally fraternity, and there was no bigger scally than Tony McGovern.

'Ready son?' asked Dad, winding down his window. As he slid into the front passenger sheet, Kev could feel his neck prickling. 'Everything all right?' asked Dad.

'Sure. Why wouldn't it be?' Well, he couldn't greet the old man with the truth, could he? *Everything's just fine Dad, considering everybody I know hates your guts.*

'So what's the big deal?'

Kev jerked his head in Gareth's direction. 'Later, eh?'

Dad glanced at his younger son, kicking his heels on the back seat. 'Later it is.'

By the time later came, Kev was having misgivings. Even two strikes didn't help. Dad handed Gareth a coke and turned to Kev.

'So what's the big secret?' he asked.

Kev took a deep breath. 'Mum,' he said, 'she's got a new feller.'

'Yes, and?'

'That's it.' Dad tossed his head back and gave a belly-laugh that turned half the heads in the bowling alley. 'What are you laughing at?'

'Carol's a big girl now,' said Dad. 'She can do as she pleases.'

'You mean you don't care?'

'I don't give a monkey's.'

Kev couldn't believe his ears. Was he going mad? Dad, he was screaming inside, this is Mum I'm talking about.

Gareth, however, looked suddenly interested. 'I like monkeys,' he said. 'Can we go to Chester Zoo?'

'Sometime son,' said Dad, humouring him.

Kev stared down at the floor. He'd planned for all sorts of reactions: anger, sadness, even a need to go round and knock Jack Dougan's block off. But not indifference. 'I thought you'd go mad.'

'Then you thought wrong,' said Dad. 'Me and your mum, we're ancient history. It's about time Carol got herself somebody new.'

Kev felt deflated. He wasn't sure what he'd expected. A rekindling of the flame, maybe. 'I thought . . .'

'What, that I'd go round and start shouting the odds? Forget it, lad. Any feelings we had for each other are . . .'

'History?'

Dad smiled humourlessly. 'That's about it.'

'You're mad!' cried Kev, his eyes stinging 'What's the matter with you, Dad? Don't you care about us?' Dad frowned. 'No,' said Kev bitterly, 'you don't give a monkey's, do you?'

With a long sigh, Dad tried to placate Kev. 'So what do you want me to say?'

Dozens of possible answers rushed though Kev's mind. That you love her. That you want us to be a family again. That you'll never let another man near

Mum. But he didn't say any of them. He was stunned to silence.

But Gareth wasn't. 'He's a policeman,' he announced.

'Come again?' Dad's expression changed suddenly. He was interested now, all right.

'Mum's boyfriend, he's a copper.' Kev stared at Gareth. He'd been wondering how to spill this particular bean. Now his younger brother had done it for him.

'Is this true?' asked Dad.

Oh, we've got your attention now, all right, thought Kev. 'Yes, it's true.'

'And what does he do in the police?'

'I've never asked.'

'Then ask.'

'Why?'

'Because,' Dad told him, 'our paths might cross, and I don't want him having anything on me.'

'It's Mum he's interested in,' said Kev.

'Maybe,' said Dad. 'Sly beggars, these coppers. So what's his name?' Dad took a sip of Coke.

'Jack,' said Kev.

Dad nearly choked. 'Jack?,' he croaked. 'Not Jack Dougan?' There was a noticeable twitch in his cheek.

'That's right,' said Kev. 'Is something wrong?'

'That's an understatement, if ever there was one. Jack Dougan's the new kid on the block, a rising star. He's set himself this cute little ambition in life; he wants to put me and Lee away.' There was something in Dad's voice. It couldn't be. Was he afraid? Whatever Dad was, Kev couldn't bear the idea of losing him again. He looked Dad in the eye.

'But he won't . . . will he?'

Dad laughed. A hollow laugh. 'Over my dead body.'

Eight

It's a crunch week for the Diamonds. Crunch week for me too, maybe. Tomorrow morning we face St Patrick's Thistle, the side sitting just above us in the table. They beat us last time out one-nil, but we ought to be able to get our own back. There's just one problem; we've only won one in five, hardly the form of championship contenders, and morale couldn't be much worse. The team's got more cracks than my bedroom ceiling. I could throttle Conor. Liam's been bending over backwards, trying to get him to settle into the team. But will old big-mouth have any? No way. Don't they realize? If we lose this one, we can kiss the title goodbye. All the effort I've put in and my mates seem hell-bent on throwing it away. Have they gone mad?

Maybe it isn't only the game that's getting to me. I've been on tenterhooks all week over Mum and Dad. We're coming to the end of something, I can feel it. It's not like the good times have all gone or anything. They weren't that great to begin with. But a crossroads has been reached and the future scares me witless. I've never liked Mum and Dad being separated, but I live with it. At least they are both around. The last week's really got me thinking though. It's this Dougan feller. It isn't true, is it? He couldn't take Mum away. He couldn't get Dad sent down. Until now I've thought my parents were invincible. Mum's always there. As for Dad, he's fireproof, isn't he? But all that's changing. It's like Mum's never home and Dad's rattled. He seems scared, actually scared of Dougan. There were plenty of brave words when I challenged him over this copper, but I'm not sure Dad believed them himself. I'd feel happier if

Dad was worried enough to lie low, but that's something he just can't do. Sooner or later it will all get too much for him. Then he'll come looking for Dougan.

This is bad news, Kev lad, it's all falling apart.

Nine

Another Sunday morning and the Diamonds were once more at each other's throats. Daz strode forward hugging the ball and screamed at his defenders. 'Step up, for crying out loud. You're making it easier for them.' There were sheepish looks from Chris and Ant. They'd been under pressure from the start and St Pat's were exploiting the space the Diamonds were allowing them.

'This isn't working,' said Kev. His heart had sunk when Ronnie told them he was persisting in playing him up front, this time partnering Conor. The opening exchanges confirmed his doubts. St Pat's were all over them and the jittery Diamonds defenders were losing possession through a string of unforced errors.

'Come on, lads,' shouted Liam, needled by his team mates' sluggish performance. Aware of his dad on the touch-line, he was determined to bury the wimp tag. Kev smiled. Liam's form was an encouraging sign. At least there was one player who wanted to take the game to the enemy. Unfortunately, Liam was still being frozen out by Ant and Joey. He was having to drop deep looking for the ball.

'Hold on to the thing for goodness' sake,' Ronnie was shouting from the touch-line. 'Place your passes. It's like watching pinball. Get your act together. Joey, get it down the line.' But Joey wasn't on his wavelength. He listlessly allowed the ball to run off his boot and out of play. Ronnie threw up his arms in disgust. The throw-in gave him more anguish. 'Pick up these loose players,' he yelled. 'John, Peter, look alive, will you?'

But St Pat's were sharp and incisive. They were knocking the ball about neatly, forcing the Diamonds to chase the game. Kev tried to catch Ronnie's eye. He was wasted hanging round in the St Pat's half. 'Joey, Ant,' bawled Ronnie. '*Anybody*, close him down.' The St Pat's winger Frankie Hall was giving him cause for concern. He was quick and he'd already shown an appetite for stinging attempts on goal. As if to emphasize the scale of the threat he posed, Hall left Joey for dead and surged forward to the corner of the area before whipping it across the goal-mouth.

'Clear it,' cried Ronnie. 'Clear the flaming thing.' His pleas went unheeded. Ant took a desperate swing at the ball only to knock it clumsily to the feet of St Pat's striker Mike Dalby. A half-volley and the Diamonds' defence was breached. Nil-one.

'Oh, great,' groaned Kev. 'Behind again.'

'Garbage, aren't they?' said Conor, gesturing towards the bickering back four.

'What's this *they*?' asked Kev.

'The defence,' said Conor hastily, trying to cover himself.

'You know what, Conor,' said Kev tetchily, 'the sooner you realize you're part of this team the better. No stars in this side, lad. Either you're a Diamond or you're not.'

'Of course I'm a Diamond,' said Conor, shaken for once. 'I didn't mean it the way you think.'

Kev walked away. 'Didn't you?'

The match continued in much the same fashion; St Pat's quick and lively, the Diamonds lethargic and second-best in most areas of the field.

'This is chronic, Guv,' said Liam. 'We've got to ring the changes.'

'Tell me something I don't know,' said Kev. His voice was little more than a whisper. He was choking on his own disappointment. 'Listen Liam, you're about the only one who looks up for this. The moment you get the ball no fancy stuff. Get it forward. Route one.'

'Got it.'

St Pat's were pressing again. Frankie Hall was sweeping down the wing. Skipping past Ant's challenge, he unleashed a stinging shot that rattled the crossbar. 'I thought that was in,' said Kev, his heart hammering. Two minutes later the Diamonds launched their first attack for some time. Ratso broke free of St Pat's tight marking and stroked it wide to Joey.

'My ball,' shouted Liam. Spotting Ronnie watching him, Joey fed him an accurate pass. Liam pounced on it gleefully and set off like a locomotive.

'That's it, Liam,' shouted Ronnie. 'Go on, lad, run it.' That one morsel of encouragement was all Liam needed. He felt a burst of energy and powered past the two defenders ahead of him.

'Cross it, Liam,' screamed Kev racing in, 'now!' Liam cut in, steadied himself and struck the ball low and hard. Skipping dangerously across the greasy turf, it picked up pace and found Conor lurking at the far post. One-all.

Kev stood, hands on hips, grinning broadly. 'Now

that,' he observed, admiring the opportunism, 'is what I call a striker's goal. No service for twenty-five minutes and he converts the only chance he gets. Peach, Conor, peach.'

Conor was hardly mobbed by his team mates. In fact, but for his dad's shouted encouragement, he celebrated alone. Liam kept his distance. Dad was making a fuss about the goal, but he seemed to have forgotten all about the cross. Typical. Liam wished Kev had got on the end of it instead.

'Let's hope that's a springboard,' said Liam. Kev nodded. Unfortunately, that one goal completely against the run of play turned out to be the Diamonds' only purposeful attack of the half. The game settled into a grim stalemate in mid-field that was finally ended by the half-time whistle. One-all.

'Lucky isn't in it,' said Ronnie. 'We ought to be three down and somehow we're level.'

'Luck,' snorted Conor. 'Skill, more like it.' Liam looked around. Ant was speechless with rage. True to form, Conor had said the wrong thing at exactly the wrong time. He'd certainly upset Ronnie.

'Oh, I quite agree with you,' the manager said. 'It was skill, all right – Liam's. That run of his was the one decent thing we did all half.'

Good speech, thought Liam. Pity it didn't come from Dad. He was too busy inspecting his watch. Something about having to go early to help a mate with his fence. Joey and Daz didn't enjoy Ronnie's speech though, and looked away in disgust.

'Oh, it's no good turning your noses up, you two,' said Ronnie. 'I mean exactly what I say. There's no fluency or coherence to our play, particularly on the left.'

'So what do you intend to do about it?' asked Kev.

'Radical surgery,' said Ronnie. 'Joey, you're off.'

'Me? How come?'

'Easy lad,' said Ronnie. 'I told you to give Liam some of the ball, but would you listen? One pass, that's all you managed and that was because I had my beady eye on you. One lousy pass. So that's it, you're off. Dougie, you've got your chance. You're playing left back. Play your heart out, lad.'

'You've got to be joking,' Daz protested, leaping to his mate's defence. 'Joey's twice the player Dougie is.'

'Tough,' said Ronnie belligerently. 'My mind's made up. I want players who'll work their guts out for the team. Got that? Not for themselves, not for their best mates, for *the team*. Come on Joey, hand on heart, can you honestly tell me you've been doing that?'

Joey glanced at Daz, then hung his head. 'No.'

'Kevin, you're back in mid-field.' The news had Kev beaming from ear to ear. 'I owe it to you son. I've been playing you out of position and we've paid for it. I'm not going to take you out of mid-field again.'

'So what are we going to do about the attack?'

Ronnie looked around the team. He wasn't exactly blessed with options. 'Liam,' he said finally. 'You partner Conor up front.' Liam's head snapped round. 'Got a problem, Liam?'

Yes, thought Liam, my moron of a brother, though he didn't say that. Just a mumbled: 'No.'

'Right lads,' said Ronnie, trying to finish the team talk on an upbeat note. 'Take the game to them.'

Bashir was accompanying Kev on to the field when

he stopped dead. 'Twice in a week,' he said. 'I wonder what's going on.'

Kev frowned. 'What are you on about, Bash?'

Bashir pointed towards Jacob's Lane. 'He's turned up again.'

'Dad,' exclaimed a surprised Kev. 'What's he doing here?' Bashir shrugged and made his way to his position out on the left. Kev hung on for Dad. 'What gives?' asked Kev.

'I've come to watch you play.'

Kev noticed that Dad was breathing heavily, like he'd been running. 'Why?'

'I'm your dad, aren't I? Do I need a reason?'

'You do when it's the first time you've come to see me in months.' Dad glanced nervously towards Jacob's Lane. 'Is something wrong?' asked Kev.

'Of course not. Why?'

Kev heard a police-car siren wailing in the distance. Then another. From the direction of the Diamond came a thick pall of smoke. 'That hasn't got anything to do with you, has it?' Kev asked doubtfully.

'Don't be daft,' said Dad. 'What a suspicious mind you've got. Go on, lad. Show me what you're made of.' Kev was turning to go when Dad spoke up again. 'There is one thing,' said Dad. 'If Jack Dougan happens to ask about me, I was here for the whole game.' Kev stiffened. Dad coming to see him play? He knew it was too good to be true.

'What did he want? asked Bashir.

'He's come to see me play,' said Kev. Bashir's querying gaze made him feel uneasy. 'I know,' Kev said hurriedly. 'I was surprised.'

The Diamonds hardly started the second half fired-up. Eager to turn their lion's share of possession into goals, St Pat's were pressing from the off. First Robbie Weaver shot into the side netting. Then Daz tipped over a good effort from Tommy Sinclair.

'Come on, Diamonds,' shouted Ronnie, dismayed by the sluggish start. 'Kev get them moving, will you?' It was easier said than done. Kev could smell the acrid smoke drifting in from the Diamond. Just what had Dad been up to? Kev was finding it hard to get himself moving, never mind the rest of the team and Dad's presence was making it even more difficult to concentrate.

'Get a grip, Diamonds,' shouted Ronnie, more in hope than expectation. But a minute later St Pat's had his side on the rack yet again. This time Daz failed to hold a powerful shot along the ground, letting it squirt loose in the six-yard box. To the keeper's relief Frankie Hall was unable to get a clean shot on goal and Dougie hooked it clear.

'Kevin,' yelled Ronnie. 'What's happening? This is worse than the first half.' The shout finally alerted Kev to the threat of a demoralizing defeat. Forcing thoughts of Dad to the back of his mind he set about organizing the Diamonds.

'Chris, Ant,' he shouted. 'Push up. The back four are defending too deep. We're inviting them in. John, Ratso, you've got to get closer to your man. Now fight for every ball.' Kev certainly rallied his troops, but St Pat's didn't fold. They rose to the challenge. The result was a ten-minute skirmish for control of mid-field. Neither side managed to carve out a clear-cut chance. After booting a speculative forward ball by St Pat's captain Steve Pearce into touch, Kev almost ran into Liam.

'I know, I know,' panted Kev, thinking Liam was staring at him. 'I'm trying to give you some service.' But Liam hardly heard him. He was actually looking past Kev. The match was turning out to be a tale of two dads, and his was shouting goodbye.

'Got to get off,' his dad shouted. 'Graham will be wondering where I've got to. Good goal, Con.'

Great, thought Liam, he gets all the praise as usual.

Still the Diamonds failed to raise their game. They were disjointed, playing in small groups rather than as a team, and it was St Pat's who rediscovered their attacking sharpness. First Sean Holder then Frankie Hall went close, before Tommy Sinclair almost put his side ahead with a shot that bobbled dangerously in front of Daz. It was Dougie who eventually got it clear, earning an enthusiastic thumbs-up from Ronnie.

'You're playing to your brief, Dougie lad,' he shouted. 'Brilliant.' Positively glowing with the compliment, Dougie slipped the ball through to Jimmy. Driving forward, he spotted Bashir in space out on the left and found him with an inch perfect cross-field ball.

'Go on, Bash,' cried Kev. 'Centre it.' At last the Diamonds produced a move in keeping with their pedigree. John met Bashir's cross and touched it on to Ratso. He fired the ball in towards a stationary Conor. Fortunately for the Diamonds Liam was alive to the possibilities and barged through two tackles before giving the St Pat's keeper no chance with a right foot finish from six yards out.

'Goal!' bellowed Kev, as he and Bashir congratulated Liam. Somehow, Liam couldn't enjoy the goal that much. For starters, most of the team ignored him. More depressingly still, his dad was long gone.

Ten

Kev wanted the ground to swallow him up. What was Dad up to? There he was in brand new Dockers and tan leather jacket acting the proud father.

'That's my boy,' he was boasting to Ratso's dad. 'He was good in the first half, but that second half performance. Cracker.'

'What's he on about, Guv?' said Bashir. 'He wasn't even here for the first half.'

'He wants everybody to think he was,' murmured Kev absentmindedly. He was looking at Dad's new gear and wondering why he didn't think of throwing something his way.

'What was that?'

'Oh, nothing.' Kev looked around him. Conor and Liam had already gone – separately. Their enforced striking partnership hadn't really worked. If Ronnie had been expecting telepathy, he'd been bitterly disappointed. They'd played alongside each other, but certainly not together. Joey had also left early, upset at being substituted. Daz, of course, had followed him.

'I tell you what, Guv,' said Ratso, wandering over. 'We didn't deserve to win.'

Kev continued to watch Dad loudly announcing his presence. He wanted everybody to know he'd been here, all right. 'I know.'

'Still,' said Ratso, 'Remember the old cliché.'

'And what's that, Rats?'

'Playing badly and still coming away with the points is the sign of a good side.'

'Oh yeah, right.' Kev was unimpressed.

'OK,' said Ratso, disappointed by Kev's reaction. 'Maybe a round-up of the other results will put a smile on your ugly mug.' He handed Kev his usual dog-eared scrap of paper.

'This kosher?' gasped Kev.

Ratso nodded. 'I thought it would cheer you up.'

'Liver Bird lost! I wondered why they hadn't been over.'

'Let's have a butchers,' said Jimmy, overhearing the glad tidings. 'Ajax drew! That's good for us. Northend drew too . . .'

'They would do,' said Ratso. 'They were playing each other.'

'Oh yes, forgot. How did Longmoor do?'

'That's the only bit of bad news,' said Kev. 'They got back into winning ways. They leap-frogged the Liver Bird into second place.'

'Hang on a minute,' said Ratso. 'I'll knock up the new league table.' While he worked the remaining Diamonds carried out their own post-mortem into the match.

'We were rubbish,' said John.

'We still climbed a place,' said Jimmy, putting the best gloss on the day's events. 'We're in fifth place.'

'Yes,' said John, 'but how many points adrift?'

'There are still six games to go,' said Chris. 'We'd be stupid to throw the towel in now.'

'He's right,' said Kev. 'There'll be no giving up while I'm captain.' Ant gave a derisive laugh. 'And what's up with you?' demanded Kev.

'Oh, you're good with the big talk,' said Ant. 'But I'd like to see some action.'

'Meaning?'

'Meaning everything started to go wrong when they joined the team.' He jabbed a finger to make his point. 'If Ronnie won't kick them out, we should do something ourselves.'

'Such as?'

'Send them to Coventry.'

'Funny,' said Kev, 'I thought that's what you'd been doing.'

'Yes, me, Joey and Daz. What about the rest of you?'

'What about us?' Kev asked hurriedly, keen to prevent anybody wading in on Ant's side. 'Have you forgotten who scored today?' Ant shuffled his feet. 'You've got no answer to that, have you?' said Kev. 'So listen up, Diamonds. We've got the makings of a team that can win the championship, maybe even a league and cup double. There's only one thing working against us, and that's ourselves.'

'Guv's right,' said Jimmy. 'We're our own worst enemy.' Ant scowled. 'I'll tell our Jamie you're all thinking about him,' he said sarcastically.

'Jamie's my mate too, you know,' said Kev.

'Oh sure,' said Ant. 'Sounds like it. That Conor breaks his wrist and you welcome him back into the team with open arms.'

Kev turned away in frustration. 'Oh, for goodness' sake . . .!' He noticed Dad hanging around behind the goal. Waiting for me, maybe, Kev thought. He nearly went over, but decided against it. In the meantime, Ratso had prevented the quarrel turning into a full-scale row.

'Here's the table,' he declared. It made interesting reading:

	Pl	W	D	L	Pts
Ajax Aintree	16	10	5	1	35
Longmoor Celtic	16	10	4	2	34
Liver Bird	16	10	3	3	33
Northend United	16	8	5	3	29
Rough Diamonds	16	8	3	5	27
St Patrick's Thistle	16	7	4	5	25

'Eight points!' exclaimed Jimmy. 'Are you sure about this, Ratso?'

'Have I ever been wrong before?'

'No, but . . . Well, I was convinced the gap would be bigger. If any of the top three slip up, we could be in.'

'Tall order,' said John dubiously.

'Maybe,' said Chris, 'but funnier things have happened.'

Kev looked around for Dad. He'd be glad of that lift. It would give him a chance to probe Dad over the morning's events. 'Bash,' he said, scanning the playing-field in vain, 'have you seen my old man?'

'He went about five minutes ago,' said Bashir. 'I thought you'd seen him.'

'Oh.' Kev was disappointed. Dad hadn't even said goodbye.

'He was with that creep,' said Bashir. 'The one who's been giving my dad a hard time over his shop.'

Kev stopped dead. 'You don't mean . . .'

Bashir nodded. 'He left with Lee Ramage. Brain Damage was there too. He must have been watching him in the Liver Bird game.' Bashir gave Kev a knowing look before delivering his killer line. 'funny how Ramage and your dad both turned up together.'

'Yes,' said Kev, his heart sinking, 'funny.'

Eleven

We kept our hopes alive against St Pat's – just. But if that was a crunch match, the next two could decide our whole season. This Sunday we play the old enemy, the Liver Bird, in the cup. Games don't come any bigger. Me and Brain Damage have been at war ever since I moved to the Diamond, and the bad blood between me and Costello goes back even further. We moved up here from the old estate within months of each other. He remembers the bad old days and he's never going to let anybody forget the time that Kev McGovern went off the rails big style. A week later it's league leaders Ajax Aintree. It's what they call a six-pointer. We win and we close the gap to five points. They win and they've got one hand on the championship trophy. That's football for you. Within seven days we could know whether we're going to be set up for a League and Cup double or whether we're going to finish the season empty-handed.

Things at home don't help. Dad and Jack Dougan came face to face last night. Dad arrived to take me and Gareth to the Everton–Newcastle game just as Dougan was getting his feet under the table. That's right, two outings on the run. Either Dad's turned over a new leaf or he was using us as an excuse to get a look at Dougan. There was a bit of verbal fencing, Dougan making out he knew what Dad had been up to last Sunday morning and Dad challenging him to do his worst. Mum looked really uncomfortable. For a moment, I thought she was going to reach for her ciggies. It's all right for her, though. I mean, she gets a choice in the matter. Unlike me. I just have to sit there while the three of them wipe their feet on my heart. Why can't life run smoothly? What's wrong with me?

PART THREE

Fighters

We didn't play like champions, but we fought like champions.

Manchester United manager
Alex Ferguson

One

By Wednesday evening the tension was really getting to the team. Kev, Bashir, Jamie, Ant and Ratso were hanging round the top of Owen Avenue, discussing the Liver Bird game – if discussion's the right word for the bad-tempered exchange.

'So when does the plaster come off, Jay?' asked Kev, gamely trying to divert attention from the splits in the team.

Jamie looked around self-consciously. It was the first time his mum had let him out for long since he broke his wrist. 'It comes off next week,' said Jamie. 'But Mum won't let me play again until it's properly healed.'

'Your old lady won't let you do anything,' said Ratso.

Jamie scowled. 'You want to know why?' he said. 'She thinks I'll get into a fight with Brain Damage or Costello. She's got a bee in her bonnet over them. I keep telling her the break was nothing to do with the gang, but she won't listen. Even when I just hang round on the pavement in front of the house she keeps coming to check on me.'

'That Conor's got a lot to answer for,' said Ant. He never missed an opportunity to stick the boot in.

'Oh, let it drop, will you?' said Kev. 'Sometimes I think you hate the twins more than you hate the opposition. This is the Liver Bird we're talking about. You do remember our worst enemies?'

'And,' Bashir added, 'the game's this Sunday.'

'Guv and Bashir are right,' said Ratso. 'We're the Cup holders, for crying out loud. We're not just defending the trophy, we're defending our honour. This is the biggest game of the season, and all you can do is slag off Conor.'

'Yes,' said Ant, unrepentant, 'and if any of you had backed me up, the Savage brothers would be history and the Diamonds would be fine. If we surrender the Cup it won't be my fault.'

'Oh, give it a rest,' snapped Kev.

'Easy for you to say,' Jamie retorted. 'You're not the one with the broken wrist. You know what Mum said to me before I went out?'

'No, what?'

'Only that she's going to do spot-checks on me, to make sure I don't hurt my arm again. There goes my freedom. See what that Conor's putting me through?'

Kev turned away. 'Are we going to argue all night?' he asked. 'Or are we going to do something?'

'Like what?' asked Ant irritably. 'There's nothing to do on this dump.'

'Some fun you are,' said Ratso. 'All you ever do is moan.'

'Keep it down, you two,' said Kev. 'We've got company.' Ant looked up. He'd been picking a fight all evening. Now he'd got one. Approaching them were Brain Damage, Costello, Tez Cronin, Carl Bain and Mattie Hughes.

'What's this, kiddies?' sneered Costello. 'A little chat to decide what to do after we knock you out of the Cup?'

'Dream on,' said Kev. 'We beat you back in August and we'll beat you again this Sunday.'

'You reckon?' said Brain Damage. 'So who's six points ahead in the League? Tell me that.'

'League position isn't everything,' said Ratso, about to embark on some of his instant punditry.

'Oh, shut up wimp,' said Brain Damage sharply, 'I'm talking to the organ grinder, not the rotten monkey.' Ratso's pinched face coloured.

'Don't tell him to shut up,' growled Kev, nettled.

'So who should I tell?' asked Brain Damage.

Kev stepped forward. 'You could try me for size.' The pair were squaring up.

'Come on then,' said Brain Damage, working himself up, 'want some, do you?' Meetings between Kev and Brain Damage had always been pretty high-octane affairs, but this one was reaching flashpoint quicker than most. Kev was about to give his answer the only way he knew, with his fists, when Jamie dug him in the ribs.

'Knock it off, Guv. Mum's coming.' Kev looked over Brain Damage's shoulder. Sure enough, Mrs Moore was approaching from the direction of South Road Community Centre.

'What's going on here?' she demanded, weighing up the situation at a glance.

'Nothing,' said Jamie.

'Nothing,' said Kev.

'Catch you later, Diamonds,' said Brain Damage.

Mrs Moore watched the gang drifting away. 'So what was all that about?'

'I told you,' Jamie replied. 'Nothing.'

'I'll give you nothing,' Mrs Moore told him. 'You're coming home with me. I told you to stay out of trouble and here you are fighting with *them*.'

'We weren't fighting,' Kev protested. 'It was just . . .'

'Kevin McGovern,' said Mrs Moore coldly, 'if I was after advice, you're the last person I'd come to.'

'Mum,' moaned Jamie. 'You're embarrassing me.'

'Oh, I'll embarrass you all right,' said Mrs Moore. 'I'll embarrass you all the way home. Now, stop arguing and get moving.'

Jamie hung his head and followed her. 'See you, lads.'

'Yes, see you Jamie.' The remaining Diamonds watched them go, then turned their attention to the game once more.

'I hate Brain Damage,' said Ant. 'He's so flaming cocky.'

'He's got reason to be,' said Ratso. 'One defeat in six games. Four back-to-back victories before last week.'

'Tell me something,' said Ant. 'Don't you ever get sick of statistics?'

Ratso grinned. 'Never.'

'It's stupid though,' said Ant. 'They don't mean anything.'

'They do, you know,' Kev corrected him. 'They mean that the Liver Bird are one of the form teams in the league. They're a different kettle of fish to the outfit we beat in the summer.'

'What about us?' asked Bashir.

'Do I need to say it?'

'Go on,' said Ant, 'you know you're dying to.'

'Let me put it like this,' said Kev. 'If we keep on playing like we have, they'll bury us.' Ratso and Bashir stared at him. It wasn't like the Guv'nor to sound so pessimistic.

'What's with you?' asked Ratso. 'You'd batter me if I said anything like that.'

'I know,' said Kev, admitting to his doubts. 'I'm worried, that's all. The Diamonds aren't the team they were.'

'My point exactly,' said Ant. 'The twins . . .'

'You don't get it, do you?' fumed Kev. 'It's things like your stupid feud with Conor that have got us into this mess. If we don't get our act together, they're going to beat us. Got that, Ant? The Liver Bird could actually turn us over. So how would you feel about that?'

'Are you trying to blame me for all this?' asked Ant, furious.

Kev wasn't in any mood to back off. 'If the cap fits . . .'

'I don't need to listen to this,' said Ant tetchily. 'I'm going home.'

'Go after him,' said Bashir, as Ant marched away. 'Patch things up.'

Kev sat down on the crumbling brick wall at the top of the Avenue. 'I will,' Kev said miserably. 'Just as soon as I can think of something to say to him.'

Two

It was Friday evening and it was as if an invisible force-field had been created between Liam and Conor. Their paths rarely crossed, and if they did scarcely a word was exchanged. Things weren't much better between Liam and Dad.

'How much longer is this going to continue?' Mum asked. Conor grimaced. Liam gave a noncommital shrug of the shoulders. Unlike Conor who seemed to revel in conflict, Liam was hating every minute of their stupid vendetta. All his life, he'd always been the one to make the first move. Couldn't Conor ever admit he was wrong? Just once?

'Wonderful,' said Mum. 'Now you've lost the power of speech.'

'Give it a rest, Karen,' Dad told her. 'Brothers have rows. They'll patch it up.'

'Oh yes?' Mum broke off from the ironing. 'And when will that be? This millennium or next? Life round your house might have been one big punch-up. I wasn't brought up like that.'

Liam sighed. It always came down to this. Dad came from a big, rough-and-ready Everton household where the kids had to scrap for attention. Mum was an only child from the Crosby suburbs. They obviously loved each other, but they really were from different galaxies. Talk about the attraction of opposites!

'They'll get over it,' Dad insisted. 'Just as soon as they get fed up sulking.'

Stung by Dad's comment, Conor piped up. 'I'm not sulking.'

'No,' said Dad, 'of course you're not. Let me guess, it's a sponsored grump.' Conor scowled and stamped upstairs.

'Well done, Lenny,' said Mum, 'you handled that well.'

'I only said they'd get fed up of sulking,' Dad retorted.

'I'm *not* sulking!' muttered Liam, before heading for the door himself. He had his own reasons to snap at Dad. He was so angry he caught his arm on the door.

'Are you all right?' asked Dad.

'Of course I'm all right,' Liam retorted. '*What do you think I am – a wimp?*'

Dad snapped round. 'Oh, you're not still going on about that, are you? I didn't mean anything.'

'Then why say it?' snarled Liam.

'Well, let's face it,' said Dad. 'You're hardly SAS material, are you?' Liam gave a strangled cry and slammed the door behind him. This time Mum didn't say a word. She simply held out her arms, palms facing out in a gesture of despair.

Now where? thought Liam, resting his back against the living room door. *Conor's* upstairs. *Dad's* in the living room. That leaves the kitchen or the bathroom. Great choice. It was the kitchen that finally got the verdict. Liam got a pot noodle and a ring doughnut out of the cupboard. 'May as well stuff myself,' he said out loud. 'There's nothing else to do.' He couldn't believe it. He was actually missing getting battered on the Gamestation. Before he had a chance to peel the top of the pot noodle, the phone rang. 'I'll get it,' he called. Nobody answered. It was that sort of house this Friday evening. 'Hello.' It was Ronnie.

'Is that Liam or Conor?' he asked.

'Liam.'

'I'm just phoning to see if you're OK for Sunday,' said Ronnie.

'Of course I am. What gives? You don't usually phone to remind us.'

Ronnie hesitated. 'I don't need to spell it out, do I?' he said after a couple of moments, 'I just wanted to make sure you weren't put off. Some of the lads have been giving you a pretty hard time.'

'I've had worse.' He had too. With a brother like Conor, you got used to it.

'Sure?'

'Sure I'm sure.'

'Fair enough,' said Ronnie. 'Can you put Conor on?'

Liam went into the living room. 'Dad,' he said, 'call Conor. Ronnie wants him on the phone.'

'Oh behave,' said Dad. 'Call him yourself.'

'No way,' said Liam.

Shaking his head in frustration, Dad called up to Conor. 'Ronnie's on the phone.' Liam listened as Conor went through the same conversation he'd just had. The moment he hung up, Conor retreated back upstairs. 'How long *is* this going to carry on?' Dad asked. 'Now it's getting on my nerves too.'

'Told you,' said Mum, delighted to have scored a point. Liam crossed his arms and fixed his eyes on the television. 'Enjoying it?' asked Mum.

'It's all right,' said Liam.

'So how long have you been interested in building a rockery garden?' Liam ignored her and continued to stare at the screen.

'I'm cheesed off,' said Dad. 'I'm going to take a run up to Crosby Marina. You know, watch the sunset, collect shells, run through the sand dunes. Anybody game?'

'Not tonight,' said Mum, 'I've got piles of ironing.'

'Coming Liam?' asked Dad. Liam ignored him. 'Oh, give over sulking, will you?' Dad walked into the hall and called upstairs.

'Conor, we're going to Crosby. Do you want to come?'

'Be there in a second.' When Conor appeared at the top of the stairs he spotted Liam at the bottom. 'He isn't coming, is he?'

'I've asked him.'

'Then I'm staying.'

'For goodness' sake!'

'I told you,' Conor insisted. 'I'm not going anywhere with him.'

'That goes for me too,' said Liam.

'Look,' said Dad. 'This is daft. You're cutting off your nose to spite your face.'

'Then,' said Liam, marching back into the living room, 'I'll do without the nose.' It was only when he had dropped back into his chair that he realized how stupid that sounded. This thing with Conor, it was getting out of hand. You know what, Liam thought to himself, it's gone far enough.

Three

Kev arrived home, his quarrel with Ant still ringing in his ears, only to walk in on a row between Mum and Dad. Noticing Gareth cowering apprehensively at the bottom of the stairs, he sat down beside him and listened to the raised voices in the living room. The door was open and he could see Mum and Dad facing each other.

'How long's this been going on?' Kev asked, as Dad thumped his fist down on the coffee table. Gareth shrugged his shoulders. His eyes were brimming with tears and his lip was trembling. There was no point upsetting him further. A choc-ice was melting on the stair carpet. If Gareth couldn't finish an ice-cream, the row must be bad!

'Don't come round to *my* house shouting the odds, Tony McGovern,' Mum yelled.

'And what do you expect me to do, Carol?' Dad roared back. 'Dougan. Jack flaming Dougan! Do you know who he is, woman?'

'He's a kind, gentle man . . .'

Mum stopped dead. 'What am I explaining myself to you for? It's none of your business.'

'It is when he's set his heart on sending me down.'

'Then maybe,' Mum spat back, 'you shouldn't give him any excuse. Or did you miss the word *honesty* when you were at school?' Dad glared at her, but didn't attempt a reply. 'What do you expect, Tony? Jack's a copper. You're a . . .' She stopped short of spelling it out when Kev and Gareth were in earshot. 'It's just the way things go.'

'You don't have to encourage him.'

'Meaning?'

'Oh, don't act stupid, Carol,' Dad seethed. 'You're seeing a man who wants to put me inside.'

Mum wasn't backing off: 'I didn't know I needed your permission,' she said. 'I thought you'd given up any claim on me when you cleared out.'

'You don't get it, do you?' Dad said. 'We do things differently round here. We don't grass and we don't go with coppers.'

'Who's grassing?' Mum asked angrily.

'Don't try to tell me you don't talk about me.'

'You've been mentioned, yes,' said Mum. 'But only as the father of my boys. I think Jack's as embarrassed by this as I am.'

'Oh, so I'm an embarrassment, am I?'

Mum mused on this for a moment. 'Frankly Tony, yes. What sort of example are you setting Kev and Gareth?'

Dad moved out of sight. He was quiet for a few moments, then his voice fairly cracked across the room. 'Well, talk of the Devil! If it isn't old flatfoot himself!'

Mum followed Dad to the window. 'Jack.' There was

another pause then Mum spoke again. 'Don't cause a scene Tony, please.'

Kev took Gareth's arm. 'Come on, mate,' he said with unaccustomed gentleness. 'This is no place for you.' He installed Gareth in his room with his Battlestar and walked back to the top of the stairs. He saw Mum greeting Dougan at the front door. There were some whispered words then a snatch of conversation Kev could hear.

'I'd better go.'

'No, you stay,' said Mum. 'It's Tony who'll have to leave.'

Dougan glanced round. 'Looks like somebody's waiting for him anyway.' Kev flew to the front bedroom window and peered out. Sure enough, Lee Ramage was sitting in his BMW waiting for Dad. He was giving Dougan the eye.

'Well, if it isn't DS Dougan,' said Dad, emerging from the living room.

'Hello Tony,' said Dougan. 'I see your choice of friends hasn't improved.' He indicated Ramage.

'Who I knock around with is my business, or is there a law against that now?'

Dougan gave a half-smile. 'No Tony, there's no law against that, but there's definitely one against what you were doing last Saturday and Sunday.'

'And what do you think I was doing?' Mum watched the two men uneasily.

'Let's not play games, Tony. I know exactly what was in the back of that car when you torched it. What's up, did we get too close for comfort? Is that why you had to burn the evidence?'

Dad snorted. 'I don't know what you're talking about, Dougan.'

'No,' Dougan said sarcastically. 'Of course you don't.'

Dad shoved his face into Dougan's. 'Listen Dougan, you don't like me and it's mutual, I assure you. I don't like you hanging round the taxi firm and I don't like you hanging round my wife.'

That's when Mum finally spoke. '*Your* wife!'

'That's right, Carol. My wife.'

'In word only,' said Mum.

'It makes no difference,' Dad insisted. 'In law, you're still Mrs Tony McGovern.'

'Not for long,' said Mum. 'I want that divorce, Tony and I want it ASAP.'

Kev knew that one – *As Soon As Possible*. He'd had an inkling that divorce was in the air but the news hit him like a battering ram. It was the end of a dream, that they might just patch things up. Sure, he hadn't really believed it would happen, but until that moment the door had never been completely closed. Now all hope was gone.

'I'm going to get you, McGovern,' said Dougan, his eyes narrowing. 'Nothing so certain.'

'In your dreams, Dougan,' said Dad. 'They don't call me Teflon Tony for nothing. You don't stick anything on this kiddie. Besides,' he said, a taunting grin spreading over his face, 'isn't there a rule about a copper messing about with the wife of somebody like me?'

Dad's question had penetrated Dougan's defences. His face drained of blood. 'You don't worry me, McGovern. I'm careful.'

'Not careful enough,' said Dad, pressing home his advantage. 'I'm sure your boss would be interested in what you get up to after work.' Without another word, he strode down the path towards the car. Kev couldn't let him go like that. Not after what he'd heard. Struggling with the catch to the upstairs bedroom window, he finally got it open.

'Dad,' he shouted. 'What did you come round for? Did you want to see me and Gareth?'

'That's right,' said Dad. 'But I got a bit more than I bargained for.' He glared at Mum and Dougan standing in the doorway. 'I'll be in touch, Kevin lad. Soon.'

Kev scrambled down the stairs and barged past Mum. 'Dad,' he cried. 'Hang on.'

Dad was already sitting in the driver's seat. He lowered his window. 'What's up, Kev?'

'What are you doing this for? Why are you picking a fight with him? I don't get it.' Kev gave Dougan a nervous glance and lowered his voice. 'Why can't you just keep your head down for a bit?'

Ramage laughed. 'Tony might be your dad, but you don't know him very well.'

Dad gave a wry smile. 'Lying low might make sense, but this isn't about sense. It's personal.' Then he was gone, the BMW accelerating up Owen Avenue.

'Kevin.' Mum was calling him.

'Yes?' He walked slowly up the path. In a few of the neighbours' windows, the net curtains were twitching.

'How much of that did you hear?'

'Most of it.'

'And Gareth?'

'I took him up to his room and got his toys out for him.'

'Good lad.' She hesitated for a moment. 'You shouldn't have heard us arguing like that.'

'Makes no odds,' said Kev.

'Still,' said Mum, 'that was no way to hear about the divorce.'

Kev shrugged his shoulders. 'Like I said, it makes no odds.'

Mum looked up at him, then added: 'He didn't come round to see you, you know. He hardly shows his face for months, then he's round by the minute. It isn't his family he's bothered about, it's Jack.'

'Sure,' said Kev, retreating towards his room. 'Whatever.' He reached his room and sagged onto the bed, his chest shaking with stifled sobs. Thanks Mum, you've just confirmed what Dad said. He'll never be able to steer clear of Dougan. Old memories came flooding back. Dad's last boxing match six years before and a photo in the *Echo* showing him laid out in a hall in Gateshead, the triumphant Geordie standing over him. He might call himself Teflon Tony, but no way was he invincible. He was a loser. He just didn't know it yet. The faces of Dad and Dougan revolved in his mind. It was a fight to the finish.

Four

It looks like it's true. Nothing lasts after all. Not family, that's for sure. I always knew about Dad, I suppose. The only surprise he's ever sprung wasn't that he cleared off on us, but that he was ever round at all. Now it's Mum's turn to mess up. What's she got to knock around with Dougan for? I mean, Dad's made his mistakes – one big mistake, you might say – but how can she side with his worst enemy? I didn't think she could be so stupid. She's always been the opposite of Dad. At least there was one person I could count on. Now look at her!

It looks like the Diamonds are falling apart too. It doesn't seem to matter what I do or say, we're still at each other's throats. It's like a virus – the stab-your-mate-in-the-back bug. Or should it be shoot-yourself-in-the-foot? Either way, one win against St Pat's is hardly the saving of our season. Nobody in the squad seems happy. Imagine what will happen if we lose to the Liver Bird. Make no mistake, they're up for it. Wherever I go, they're hovering, smirking and pointing like I'm some sort of joke. There was a time when I laughed at them. Not any more. With every hour that ticks by I get a worse feeling about this match. I can't help it, I just don't see any way we can win.

Five

The rain cleared just before kick-off.

'Good conditions,' said Ronnie, removing the baseball cap Gord had brought back for him from his holiday in the States. 'That shower should make the ball skip across the turf nicely.' Kev gave him a sideways look. If the state of the pitch was all he could talk about they really were in trouble.

'So who've we got to look out for?' asked Kev as the team trudged towards the pitch. 'You didn't say much in the dressing room.'

'To be honest,' said Ronnie, drawing Kev to one side, 'I didn't want to say much. The way some of the lads are at the moment, anything seems to set them off.'

'So you'd rather say nothing at all?'

Ronnie scratched his nose. 'That's about the size of it.'

Kev eyed the Liver Bird jogging onto the pitch in their all-red strip. They looked confident, intimidating even. 'Who's the tall lad?' he asked. 'I don't recognize him.'

'He's new,' said Ronnie. 'Only played one game. I can't remember his name.'

'I can,' said Ratso, who'd been eavesdropping. 'It's a corker.'

'Go on,' said Kev. 'You're dying to tell.'

'You're not going to believe it,' said Ratso, already giggling at the information he was about to impart, 'but he's called Wayne Bowe.'

'Wayne Bowe?' Kev repeated. 'Behave. Nobody's called Wayne Bowe. You're making it up.'

'I don't see why,' said Ronnie. 'I once went out with a girl called Annette Curtain.'

'Never!'

'Straight up. Nervous type she was. Always looked a bit drawn. I told her to pull herself together.'

Kev pulled a face. 'Ha hardy ha.'

'I'm not making it up about Wayne Bowe,' Ratso insisted. 'It really is his name. He's Mattie Hughes' cousin. Useful too, by all accounts. Plays as a striker. Hey Guv . . .'

Ratso leaned across, all conspiratorial. 'What?'

'Wait till you hear the music I've got.' As the Liver Bird warmed up, he slipped the cassette into his ghetto blaster. A moment later the song was blasting all round Jacob's Lane playing fields: *I can sing a rainbow*. 'Just look at his face.' Wayne Bowe was blushing bright red. The moment the rest of the Diamonds were let in on the joke, they were roaring fit to burst and adding to his embarassment.

'I'm going to bury you for that,' he warned them.

'Aw, what's up?' asked Kev, delighted to see the pleasure on his team mates' faces. 'Got no sense of humour?' It was the first time he'd felt the slightest morsel of confidence. First blood to the Diamonds, even if it was such a lame joke.

'I hope you don't think a cheap trick like that's going to help you,' said Costello, meeting Kev in the centre circle to toss for kick-off.

'We don't need tricks to beat a shower like you,' said Kev, but as the coin spun in the air, he was acutely aware of how empty his brave words were.

'Our kick-off,' said Costello. 'I'm going to enjoy this McGovern.' Kev looked round the field. Ronnie was playing the side that had finished against St Pat's, pairing the twins up front as the strike partnership. He saw Liam approach his brother, but Conor turned away. At least one of them is making an effort, thought Kev.

'Come on lads,' Kev shouted encouragingly. 'This is the match of the season. We're defending the Challenge Cup, remember.'

As Costello rolled the ball to Brain Damage, Bashir whispered something in Kev's ear. 'If we were playing like a team,' he said, 'you wouldn't have to remind us.'

Kev nodded grimly. 'I know.'

Twice in the first five minutes the Liver Bird benefitted from a lack of understanding on the Diamonds' left flank to hit their opponents on the break. First, Jelly Wobble booted the ball downfield, putting Wayne Bowe clear. Only Daz's speed off the line prevented them going behind. Less than a minute later it was Bowe again who turned the Diamonds' defence. This time Jimmy was there to clear his lines.

'Joey, Ant,' shouted Kev. 'What's going on? You've no excuse this time. Liam isn't even on the wing. Get the ball to Bashir.'

But the poor passing continued. It's as if they'd got so used to giving the ball away, they couldn't break the habit. The pressure from the Liver Bird continued. Twice Kev was on hand to dispossess Costello in the final third. But when he was cut out of the play by a tremendous crossfield pass by Mick Gavin, Kev could only watch in agony as Wayne Bowe scored from an acute angle.

'There,' said Bowe. 'Still laughing at my name?'

Even when the Diamonds put together a decent attack it invariably broke down as soon as the twins got involved. They just weren't on the same wavelength. Either they played it short or hefted it out of play altogether.

'What's the opposite of telepathy?' asked Kev.

'Dunno,' said Conor. 'Why?'

'Because that's what you and Liam have got.' If Kev's remark was meant to shame the twins into action, it seemed to have the opposite effect, Conor twice overhitting the through-ball to Liam.

'What do you call that?' demanded a red-faced Liam as the ball ran out for a goal kick. Conor shrugged nonchalantly. 'I asked you a question,' said Liam, tugging at his brother's shirt sleeve.

'Get off, you,' warned Conor, 'Or I'll . . .'

'Or you'll what?'

'Now now, Diamonds,' said Costello gleefully. 'Don't fight among yourselves.'

The remark didn't have any effect on Conor, but

Liam looked suddenly thoughtful. Two minutes later the Liver Bird had even more to gloat about. Ant committed himself to a challenge on Carl Bain. Skipping over the telegraphed tackle, Bain looked up and located Wayne Bowe racing into the box. Rising above Chris Power, the Liver Bird striker nodded it down to the feet of Brain Damage. Two-nil to the Liver Bird.

'Bit of a choker, eh?' taunted Costello. 'It's a killer when you concede just before half-time.' Kev wanted to ram Costello's words down his throat, but as he looked round his dispirited team one thing was obvious. They had the ring of truth.

Six

The Diamonds weren't looking forward to the half-time pep talk. With good reason. Ronnie was furious.

'Chronic,' he said, 'absolutely flipping chronic.' Liam looked around. Nobody was arguing. 'Do you really want me to list our failings?' asked Ronnie. 'The back four are getting caught square, the mid-field aren't battling. As for the attack . . .' He let his arms flop against his sides. Enough said. 'I don't get it,' he said. 'The talent's there. You've got pace, skill, power. There's just one thing lacking, teamwork. I don't know what's going wrong. You were always so hungry for success. It's like you hate each other's guts.'

Right on cue Ant and Conor exchanged hostile glances while Joey's eyes burned into Liam. Is this what I've been doing? Liam thought. Is that how I've been acting?

'You've heard all this before, lads. For goodness' sake, what does it take to make you play for each other?'

'A miracle,' Liam mumbled under his breath.

'What was that?'

Liam blushed. 'Nothing, Ronnie.' But if a miracle was what was needed, a miracle he was going to produce.

'Come on, lads,' Ronnie urged. 'This is the Liver Bird you're playing. You're not telling me you're going to go down without a fight. Where's your pride?' It was a good question, and judging from the look on their faces none of the Diamonds had an answer.

'Liam,' said Kev, 'can I have a word?'

'Sure,' said Liam, 'what's up?'

'You and Conor,' said Kev. 'Is there *any* chance of sorting yourselves out?'

Liam held out both hands. 'Beats me,' he said. 'I'm ready to make an effort. Con just doesn't want to know.'

'Takes two to tango,' observed Kev. Liam took the comment on the chin. He'd been no angel in all this.

'Well?' asked Ronnie still trying to rally the troops. 'Are you going to make a fight of it, or what?' In reply, the team could manage no more than a dull murmur.

'Ronnie should have saved his breath,' said a despairing John O'Hara.

The first ten minutes of the second half were a scrappy affair, long balls, up-and-unders and plenty of inconclusive head tennis. It was a game that suited defences. Fine for the side in the lead, but desperate for the Diamonds.

'It's better than conceding another goal,' said Chris Power.

'Not much,' said Kev. 'I want to win this.' It didn't

look like anybody else did. Daz twice had his defence under pressure with poorly kicked clearances and Jimmy almost put the ball through his own net. The Diamonds finally cracked when Costello found Wayne Bowe with a telling pass. Bowe skipped past a flat-footed Joey Bannen and slotted the ball past Daz.

'Three-nil!' cried Kev. 'What do you think you're playing at, Joey? I could have stopped him with my eyes shut.'

'So why didn't you?' asked Joey. Kev walked away, shaking his head. He was aware of the mocking jeers of the Liver Bird.

'What's the score, McGovern?' Brain Damage was calling.

'Come on, McGovern,' Costello added. 'Cat got your tongue?'

'Ignore them,' said Liam.

'I'm trying,' Kev replied. 'But it isn't easy.' The Diamonds responded by going forward in numbers. Stung by the scoreline, John, Kev and Ratso had given up any defensive role and were forcing the Liver Bird back deep into their own half. At first there was little penetration as they ran up against a well-organized and very physical Liver Bird defence. But as they camped inside the opposition half, the cracks began to appear.

'Bashir,' shouted Liam as the winger scampered past his marker, 'cross it.' A deep cross found Conor and Liam drove expectantly into the area. But instead of heading the ball on to his brother, Conor chose the harder option of chesting it down and hitting the ball on the half-volley. Liam made a beeline for him.

'Now I suppose you're going to bawl me out,' Conor said.

'Not exactly,' said Liam. 'Listen Con, I've had it with

—— 113 ——

this stupid row. Let's call it quits and turn this team round.' Conor didn't answer. He just walked away without answering.

'Oh well,' said Kev, resting a hand on Liam's shoulder, 'at least you tried.' As play resumed, Liam won possession just outside the area and started to make progress, only to be hacked down by Costello.

'You animal,' cried Liam, still lying on the ground. Alerted to the flare-up, the ref whistled.

'Don't call me an animal,' said Costello, stamping on Liam's ankle. Liam responded by lashing out with his foot. 'I'll teach you to take a pop at me,' Costello bawled, as if he were the innocent party. Another blast of the whistle. With more bad-tempered exchanges erupting, the ref was struggling to maintain control. He didn't see Costello measuring up to take another kick at Liam.

'Back off,' said Conor stepping up to confront Costello. 'That's my brother.' Liam could hardly believe his eyes. *Conor* defending *him*.

'Knock it off,' the ref shouted at the mayhem in front of him. 'Who started this?'

'Those two,' said Costello. 'They were fighting then they started on me.'

'Oh yeah, sure,' said Conor, completely unperturbed. 'Like I'm going to hit my own brother.'

The ref eyed them dubiously. 'Play on,' he said after a moment's consideration, 'but no more rough stuff. OK?'

'Sure,' said Liam. 'Whatever.'

Costello gave the twins a threatening look. 'You haven't heard the last of this,' he warned.

'Look at me,' said Liam, 'I'm shaking in my boots.' As the players filtered out of the Liver Bird penalty area, he caught up with Conor. 'So what's come over you all of a sudden?'

'I've been thinking about what you said,' Conor answered. 'I've been a prat.' Without another word, Conor was gone. Liam watched him challenging the Liver Bird keeper. All that grief and suddenly Conor was declaring a truce, and doing it as if nothing had happened. Still, at least they were pulling together again. 'What are you hanging round there for?' asked Conor as he returned from baiting the Liver Bird keeper. 'We've got a game to salvage.' Liam grinned in spite of himself. If there was one thing Conor had in abundance, it was cheek.

Suddenly it was one-way traffic as the Diamonds swept forward, forcing the Liver Bird into a series of desperate last-gasp tackles to keep their three-goal margin intact.

'More like it,' said Kev, as first Conor, then Liam went close with powerful shots. It was Conor who got on the score sheet with ten minutes to go. Liam rose to meet an inswinging corner from Bashir. Spotting Conor at the near post, he headed it down to his feet. One-three.

'Get off!' roared Conor as John and Ratso ran to congratulate him. 'No time for that. Get it back to the centre spot.' Snatching the ball out of Costello's hands, Conor raced back downfield, waving the Diamonds back.

'Just look at him,' sneered Ant. 'Thinks he runs the team.'

'I'll tell you what,' said Kev, overhearing him, 'I wish we had more of that spirit.' With five minutes to go Conor returned the compliment, sliding the ball through to Liam. Steadying himself, Liam crashed the ball into the roof of the net. Two-three.

'Come on!' bawled Kev. 'We can do this.'

'*Can* do it?' said Conor. 'We're *going* to do it.'

With the Diamonds' hopes rising and the Liver Bird desperate to hang onto what they'd got, the match entered a new phase. The closing minutes of the game were as brutal as the first half had been mediocre. Carl Bain and Mattie Hughes went into the referee's book for crunching tackles on the twins and Costello was lucky to escape with a tongue-lashing for pulling Kev back on the edge of the area.

'We've got to hang on,' Costello was shrieking at his tiring troops.

'Get into them,' Kev was urging his own players. 'They're rocking.' Moments later it looked as if the Diamonds had got the breakthrough they'd been searching for. Conor ran onto Kev's pass and held off his marker long enough to slip the ball into Liam's path. Driving into the area, Liam outpaced Brain Damage and was about to shoot when Costello clattered him from behind.

'Penalty!' screamed the Diamonds. Some of them were raising their arms in celebration. But there was no whistle. The Diamonds attackers turned in disbelief.

'Ref,' pleaded Liam as he rose to his knees, 'it's got to be. Penalty.' The referee stared at him, as if still trying to make his mind up.

'Well?' Kev asked. The ref waved his arms. No penalty. Play on.

'I don't believe it,' cried Liam. 'It was blatant.' Ant and Chris were surrounding the ref.

'What's the matter with you?' demanded Ant. 'Are you blind?'

'Play on,' said the ref.

'Penalty,' said Chris. 'An obvious penalty. You can't have missed it.'

'I said,' the ref insisted stubbornly, 'play on.' If the Diamonds were still reliving the penalty controversy, the Liver Bird keeper was alive to the possiblities. Launching the ball downfield, he found Wayne Bowe.

'Get on him!' cried Kev, suddenly aware of the danger. But with most of the Diamonds defenders still preoccupied with the argument about the penalty, Bowe was left with the easiest of chances. It was four-two to the Liver Bird and Wayne Bowe's hat-trick. There wasn't even time for the Diamonds to mount an attack.

'Call yourself a referee?' cried Liam, the final whistle cutting through his heart like a rapier. 'That penalty would have been the equalizer. We've been robbed, and it's all down to you.'

'Forget it, son,' said the ref.

'Why should he?' yelled Chris Power, joining the fray. 'You've just cost us the match, you blind moron.'

'Watch your language, lad.'

'Come away, Chris,' said Liam.

But Chris had lost it. Venting his fury and humiliation at the defeat, he flung his shirt at the ref. 'You ming!' he shrieked.

'Right,' said the ref. 'I'm reporting you for that.'

Liam was trying to drag Chris away, but Chris wasn't in any mood to be helped. 'Do what you like,' he said. 'You're a disgrace, ref.'

Liam watched Chris storm off the field. 'That wasn't too clever,' he said.

'Maybe not,' said Kev. 'But at least we've started fighting again.' Liam was trying to block out the Liver

Bird jeers. As they left the pitch they were clapping
Wayne Bowe on the back and celebrating him in song:

> I can sing a Wayne Bowe
> Sing a Wayne Bowe,
> Sing a Wayne Bowe too.

Liam hung his head. Kev was doing his best to lift the
team's spirits, but at that moment they all felt shattered.
To get so close and fail at the last, it was a killer.

Seven

*I did my best. A captain's performance, you might say. But
to play your heart out and come back from the dead like
that, then lose it to appalling refereeing in the last minute,
it's too much to bear. I mean, everything was set up for a
fairy tale ending, especially when peace broke out between
the twins. Then the bad guys won after all. You should
have heard Costello and Co. They were beside themselves.
Their four-two victory was a dream come true. So there we
were, dumped out of the Cup, and by our worst enemies too.
I tried to get round the team, to lift them up off the ground.
Talk about heroics! I even surprised myself. I just wanted to
lie down and die, but I managed to talk to every player.
That's right, all the Liver Bird players were surrounding
me, jeering and taunting, rubbing my nose in the bitterness
of defeat. But I kept my head up. I got round the lads,
ordering them to pick themselves up and face Costello and
Co. Give them credit, most of the lads rose to it. The twins
really showed what they're made of, trading insults and
reminding the Liver Bird that we'd face them again in the*

League on the last day of the season. It wasn't all good news, of course. Chris has done a runner, and Ant cleared off as well. There's plenty of work to do if we're going to come back from our Cup exit and have a serious go at the League.

When the dust had finally settled and I started to think about the game, I got really depressed. Everything seemed such a mess. I got to thinking about Mum. With the Diamonds in such a state she's the only thing in my life I can rely on. I don't know what I'll do if her and Dougan decide to live together. It's just too horrible to contemplate. Oh, this is stupid. I'll bounce back. I've got to. Nobody's going to know what's going on inside me. I can't let it show. I'm the Guv'nor, after all.

Eight

Liam nearly jumped out of his skin. It was the third and final lap of 'Doomracer' and he'd never stood a better chance of beating Conor. Conor had tried every trick and cheat he'd learned in hours at the computer screen, but Liam had remained tense and focused and had never given up on the game. He'd been so intent that Mum's voice had exploded on his brain like a thunder-clap.

'Have you two seen the time?' Liam's Demon Buggy was right on the shoulder of Conor's Deathstrider. It wasn't really neck-and-neck, more skull-and-skull as they bored and jolted towards the intergalactic finishing line. Liam could hardly breathe, never mind answer. 'Liam, Conor, I thought you had training.'

'Hang on, Mum,' shouted Liam, furious at the interruption. He had the beating of Conor. Nothing, but nothing was going to get in his way this time. 'Just five minutes.'

His reply took Conor by surprise. 'Hey, that's my line.'

'And this,' cried Liam triumphantly, pounding the control pad with his fingers, 'is my game.' Conor looked back at the screen. Disbelief rushed over his face. It was true, the Demon Buggy had bounced off the banking, skipped over a laser trap and crossed the finishing line first.

'Mum put me off,' protested Conor. 'I was in front until she shouted us.'

'Yeah, yeah.'

'I was. She broke my concentration.'

'Sore loser,' said Liam, trying not to gloat. But not trying too hard, of course.

'But you never win.'

'Did this time,' said Liam, heading for the door.

'But it's impossible . . .'

'It happened though, didn't it?'

'Fluke.'

'Skill.'

Conor switched off the Gamestation. As he left his chair he glared at it, like it had betrayed him. 'Skill, *you*? I'll murder you when we get back.'

'Not if I murder you first.'

'Choose your game. I'll waste you.'

'Forget it,' said Liam, revelling in his victory. 'This is a turning point. I'm never going back. Loser no more.'

Hearing the verbal jousting, Mum met the twins at the bottom of the stairs. 'I hope this isn't what I think it is.'

'Don't worry Mum,' said Liam. 'It's just the sound of Conor moaning. I thrashed him on the Gamestation.'

'You were lucky.'

'Lucky my eye.' And that's how they straddled their bikes and pedalled off down the street, disputing the game furiously but as happy as pigs in mud. Mum permitted herself a smile. This sort of argument she could live with.

They were still at it when they turned the corner into South Road.

'Uh-oh,' said Liam. 'There's a reception committee waiting for us.' The Community Centre was a hundred yards down the bleak perimeter carriageway that was South Road, and strung across the road stood Costello, Brain Damage, Carl Bain, Tez Cronin, Jelly Wobble and Mattie Hughes.

'Here they are,' shouted Costello. 'Told you they came this way.'

'You've had it now,' Brain Damage warned the twins. 'Luke hasn't forgotten what you said to him yesterday.'

'Don't stop,' said Conor, picking up speed. 'Not for anything.' Liam followed his brother's example. As they closed on the gang, he could feel the rush of the wind and the adrenalin pumping through him. He was reliving Sunday's confrontation with Brain Damage. 'Out of the way, you sickos!' yelled Conor.

Thanks Con, thought Liam. Provoke them, why don't you? The gang's line wavered for a moment. Getting hit by a racing bike at that speed wasn't to be recommended.

'Hold your ground,' Costello told the rest of the gang. 'We've got a score to settle with them.'

'You wish,' Conor shouted back. 'You're not getting your hands on me.' He was almost down Mattie

Hughes' throat. 'One of us is going to blink,' Conor roared. 'And . . .' Mattie leaped to one side. '. . . It won't be me.' Having successfully negotiated the gang's line, Conor popped a wheelie. His celebration was shortlived.

'Con!' Liam had found himself facing Costello and Brain Damage. He'd tried Conor's tactic, but the gang leaders were made of sterner stuff than Mattie Hughes. This time Liam was the one to blink.

'Get him!' yelled Costello. 'He's the one who took a kick at me.' Veering wildly to the right, Liam lost control on the grass verge and tumbled from his bike. Costello and Brain Damage were on him in a flash. 'Not so mouthy now, are you Savage?' Costello gloated.

Liam tried to get to his feet, but pain shot through his knee. He had to content himself with a shout of protest. 'Get off.'

'That's right,' Conor said in support. 'Get off him.'

Costello smiled. A crocodile grin. 'Yesterday wasn't just a football match. It was a battle for control of the Diamond.'

'Yeah,' said Brain Damage, toe-poking Liam. 'And you lost.'

Conor had laid his bike on the pavement and was racing back to help his brother. 'Leave him alone!'

'No,' said Costello, sticking the boot into Liam's ribs. 'We won't. Now what are you going to do about it?'

'Give you a good hiding, that's what.'

Costello surveyed his troops. 'Not very good odds, are they Savage?' Liam, still lying on the ground pinned by Costello and Brain Damage, looked around. Two on to six. Not very good at all.

'Just let go of him.'

'You don't get it, do you?' said Costello. 'We're going to give you a lesson you won't forget. Something you can take back to McGovern. He isn't cock of the estate any more. He hasn't got it any more. Yesterday proved that.'

'I told you to leave Liam alone,' said Conor, making his way forward uncertainly. Liam took another kick in the ribs.

'And what if we don't?'

'Then you've got me to answer to.'

'Ooh,' mocked Brain Damage. 'You're so-o-o scary.' Costello held Liam while Brain Damage stamped on his knee. Conor didn't say anything this time. He just flew at the nearest members of the gang.

'Come on, Savage,' said Costello, his face hardening, 'I'm going to enjoy this.'

Seeing Conor wading into Tez Cronin and Jelly Wobble, Liam started to struggle with his attackers. One thought went through his mind: At least we'll go down fighting.

Twenty minutes later the enraged Diamonds were gathered round the twins.

'How many of them did you say there were?' asked Jimmy.

'Six.'

'Six on to two,' said Chris. 'Nice odds for cowards. I say we do them.' Ronnie had just informed him that he was facing a one-match suspension in a couple of weeks for his argument with the ref the day before. The punishment had done nothing to curb his aggression.

'Dad'll kill me,' said Conor, inspecting his bike.

'Don't be soft,' said Kev. 'You didn't bend that wheel. Costello and Co. did.'

'How are you feeling, Liam?' asked Gord.

Liam was hobbling up and down on his bruised knee. 'OK, I think.'

'It doesn't look OK,' said Ronnie. Jamie raised his eyes. The plaster had been taken off his wrist, but he still didn't have much sympathy for the twins.

'What are you going to do, Ron?' asked Ant. 'Run *them* to the hospital?'

'Are you trying to wind me up?' asked Conor angrily.

'I don't know what you mean,' said Ant.

'Then I'll spell it out for you. Are you telling me you're actually glad the gang turned us over?'

'We're not telling *you* anything,' said Jamie acidly. Liam was about to interrupt. He didn't want another row tearing through the Diamonds' ranks. In the event, he needn't have worried.

'An apology,' said Conor, turning towards Jamie and Ant, 'is that what you're after?'

'Wouldn't go amiss,' said Ant offhandedly.

'Then I apologize,' said Conor. 'Unreservedly. I was out of order.' He examined Jamie's face.

'So?' Jamie just stared back at him.

'Are you going to accept it?' Liam looked hopefully at Jamie.

'Sure,' said Jamie, still unsure how to respond. 'Why not?' And glanced at his cousin. He looked disappointed.

'What about you, Ant?' asked Kev. 'Ready to call a truce?'

'Yes,' said Ant grudgingly. 'Whatever.' It was hardly kiss-and-make-up, but it would have to do.

'So what are we going to do about this?' asked Ant. 'I say we go after them.'

'Me too,' said Chris. Liam looked at Conor. For the second time that evening he was pleasantly surprised.

'I think we've had enough trouble for one day,' said Conor, amazing his team-mates. 'There's only one place to settle this, on the football field.'

'First Guv, now you,' said Ant. 'How come everybody's going soft, all of a sudden?'

'Using your head isn't soft, Ant,' said Kev. 'If we'd all done it earlier, we'd still be in the Cup.'

'How do you work that out?' asked Ant.

'Easy,' said Kev. 'We've spent the last month tearing into each other. It's time we did it to the opposition.'

Ant was sticking to his guns. 'I still say we go after them.'

'You would,' said Jamie. 'I'm with Guv.' Ant stared at him in disbelief. Another recruit to the Wimp Brigade. 'He's right,' Jamie went on. 'What happened to me wasn't all Conor's fault. I played my part too. You don't get it, do you Ant? We've let ourselves down. The best thing the Diamonds had was the way we stuck up for each other and we've lost it.'

'So it's agreed?' said Kev. 'We put everything into the rest of the season?'

'Come on, lads,' said Ratso. 'We're still in with a shout. We're only eight points off the top and we play Ajax on Sunday.'

'There you go,' said Liam. 'It's an omen.'

'You what?'

'Think about it,' Liam continued, warming to his theme. 'The timing couldn't be better, could it? We've got the league leaders. It's a crunch match, a chance to show what we're made of.' John and Joey exchanged doubtful looks. 'Oh, come on,' Liam pleaded. 'For the last quarter of an hour against the Liver Bird we were magic.'

'He's right,' said Ratso. 'That's the trouble with footy. The moment the whistle blows you're blinded by the score. We lost four-two so we must have got battered. According to the experts, statistics don't lie.' He raised a finger to give weight to his argument. 'Only they do. They don't let you know all the other stuff: the refereeing decisions that go against you, the penalty that was never awarded, the shot against the bar that could have gone anywhere, the wicked deflection, the sheer bad luck . . .'

'OK, OK, Rats,' Daz interrupted. 'We get the message.'

'Look,' said Liam. 'Forget what happened in the Cup. It's what we do next that counts, and it's all set up for us. We can kill two birds with one stone; pick ourselves up after the Cup exit and put ourselves back in the title race.'

'Sounds good to me,' said Kev.

Conor grinned. 'Me too.' All eyes turned on Ant.

'Oh, fair enough,' he said. 'In for a penny, in for a pound.'

Nine

As the Diamonds warmed up for their match the following Sunday, Kev was uneasy. 'Ready lads?' he asked hopefully.

'Ready as we'll ever be,' said Daz. Kev ran his eyes over the team. They were quiet, but what did that mean? Nerves, quiet confidence? Noticing Ratso fiddling with the ghetto blaster that pounded out the Diamonds' anthems, he jogged across. 'What's the signature tune today?' asked Kev.

'This,' said Ratso. Without further ado, they ran onto the pitch to the beat of Run DMC. Ajax won the toss and elected to kick-off. Their speedy wingers Jack Hendrie and Ryan Platt were soon causing all sorts of problems, pulling Joey and Jimmy wide and exposing gaps in the Diamonds defence.

'We've got to cut the supply to those two,' Kev told his mid-field colleagues. 'Or somebody's going to get on to the end of one of their crosses.' As if to spell out the danger, Platt drove a wicked ball across the penalty area. A diving header by Chris Power stopped Daley Bennett having a free shot on goal. It was only the latest heart-stopping moment.

'John, Ratso, get out to the edge of the area,' Kev ordered. 'We're in each other's way here.' It was a wise move. When Daz punched the corner kick clear it fell at Ratso's feet. Keen to hit Ajax on the break, Ratso volleyed it upfield to Liam. Taking the ball on his chest, Liam swivelled and punted it on into the area where Conor was waiting to have a shot on goal. It took a fine diving save by Jordan Walsh to prevent the Diamonds opening the scoring. The corner provided them with another opportunity to have a strike on goal as Conor headed down for Liam to crash it against the foot of the post.

'That's it, lads,' cheered the twins' dad. He'd missed the last match against the Liver Bird. Now he was determined to make his presence felt. The supportive dad. The twins exchanged glances.

'You forgiven him yet?' asked Conor. 'You know,

over the wimp thing.' Liam shrugged his shoulders. He was talking to Dad, just not that enthusiastically. 'So it's no,' said Conor.

Liam jogged away. 'Whatever.'

'This is more like it,' Kev shouted, interrupting them. 'Good pressure. The Diamonds are back.' The point was emphasized further just two minutes later when Ratso beat two players and was squirming round a third when he was brought down a yard outside the area. 'Fancy it?' Kev asked Conor. 'It's your sort of range and it's pretty central.'

Conor weighed up the situation then winked unobtrusively. 'Nah,' he said. 'Too far out.' No sooner had the Ajax wall started to relax than Conor turned and hit the ball in one fluid movement. The rasping shot struck Ajax captain Shaun Lacey in the stomach. With a moan of pain he sank to his knees. Conor leaned over the stricken Lacey, but it wasn't to show sympathy: 'Now that,' he said, 'was pure suicide. Don't do it again, eh?' Lacey's face registered anger and bewilderment in equal measure.

'Time to turn up the heat,' said Kev.

'Better than our last meeting, isn't it?' said Ratso. 'We were three-nil down at this stage.' To prove that scoreline wasn't about to be repeated, Bashir seized on a weak clearance out of defence, drove on to the goal-line and whipped in a lethal cross. This time Conor's shot wasn't blocked and rocketed into the roof of the net. One-nil to the Diamonds.

The goal had his dad capering along the touch-line. 'Don't worry, Liam,' he called. 'You'll get one.'

'Of course I will,' said Liam offhandedly. That's how he'd been talking to Dad for a fortnight now. He didn't fly off the handle as readily as Conor, but when somebody upset him, he took some pacifying.

'Being a bit hard on him, aren't you?' said Conor. Liam gave another noncommittal shrug of the shoulders.

Ajax slowly played themselves back into the game and it was no surprise when Barry Cameron put them back on equal terms just before half-time. Kev was enraged. All that heart-pumping action and they were back to square one.

'One-all at half-time,' said Ratso. 'There's more goals in this one.'

'Better had be,' said Kev, his jaw set.

'Oh, there will be,' said Ratso. 'Mark my words. Remember how our last meeting finished. Five-all.'

'It was a good game,' said Kev. 'But a draw's no good to us today.'

'My sentiments exactly,' said Ronnie. 'We've already had enough chances to put this game out of reach. Keep playing with the same pace and confidence and we'll open them up.'

'We'll have to,' said Dougie Long, returning from a reconnaissance mission round the other pitches. 'All the other leading teams are leading.'

'You heard him,' said Ronnie. 'Take this lot to the cleaners in the second half.'

Unfortunately, it was Ajax who looked like taking the Diamonds to the cleaners. Five minutes into the second period, the Diamonds committed themselves just too far. Exploiting the space at the back, Ryan Platt set off on a scorching forty-yard run before releasing Daley Bennett. Two-one to Ajax.

'Don't let your heads drop, Diamonds,' yelled Kev as he rallied his troops. 'We've got plenty of time.'

The Ajax goal was the signal for a searing onslaught by the Diamonds front players. They ran until it felt like their lungs had been shredded. But it paid dividends. Within minutes of the restart the Diamonds were level. This time the architect was Joey, overlapping Bashir on the left and releasing Liam. A neat one-two with Conor and Liam only had to keep his head to slot the ball home from five yards.

'Goalazzo!' cried Ratso.

'Yes,' yelled the twins' dad, giving Liam the thumbs up.

Liam gave him a thin smile. 'Not bad for a wimp.' He was enjoying turning the knife. Dad had been trying to work his way into his good books for days. Liam was almost ready to forgive, *almost* being the operative word. He was determined not to make it too easy for Dad. 'Great ball,' he enthused, racing over to Joey.

'I think I owed you one,' said Joey.

Liam then jogged across to pat Conor on the shoulder. 'Even-Stevens again,' he said.

'Sure is,' said Conor. The twins were enjoying themselves.

'Here's something to wipe the smile off your faces,' said Kev. The twins looked up to see the Liver Bird players lining up on the far touch-line.

'Their match must have finished,' said Conor.

'Anybody know how they did?' asked Liam.

'No,' said Kev, 'but I'm sure they'll let us know if they won.' In the event it was a fairly subdued Liver Bird who watched the Diamonds going through their paces. Costello managed a couple of jibes, but even they were half-hearted.

'Heard the news,' Ratso panted two minutes later. 'The Liver Bird lost. Two-one to Orrell Park Rangers.'

'Brilliant,' said Conor, but not before he had raised his fingers to inform the watching Liver Bird squad that he knew they'd lost.

'Come on,' Liam urged enthusiastically. 'Let's finish this. I want to see their faces when we close the gap on them.'

First Kev, then Bashir went close with long-range shots before the Diamonds got lucky. Jordan Walsh in the Ajax goal fumbled a soft shot from John O'Hara, dropping it at Conor's feet. Conor accepted the present gleefully. Three-two to the Diamonds. Conor took a cocky bow right in front of Luke Costello. He wasn't going to miss a trick.

'You'll wish you hadn't done that, Savage,' said Costello.

Five minutes later Liam was back on terms with his strike partner. Seeing the Ajax keeper off his line he lobbed him from fifteen yards. Like Conor, he chose to celebrate smack in front of the Liver Bird. Four-two to the Diamonds. They were starting to run amok.

'You're looking a bit sick, Costello,' Liam taunted. 'Something you ate?'

When Conor sprinted through the Ajax defence to beat Walsh with a flick just inside the near-post, the result was beyond doubt and a disappointed Liver Bird team started to trail away towards the changing rooms. Only Costello and Brain Damage remained. Any retreat by them would mean losing face.

'Aw, your mates deserting you?' Kev taunted.

'Shut it McGovern,' Costello retorted. 'We hammered you, remember, and we're still above you in the League.'

'Yes,' said Conor, 'but not for long.'

'That's right,' said Kev. 'We're coming for you. See

you on the last day of the season. Call it the Armageddon match.'

'Armageddon?' asked Conor.

'Yes,' said Kev, 'Armageddon sick of those bozos.' The Liver Bird had nothing more to say, but Liam did. Not about to be overshadowed by Conor he scored right on the final whistle. Six-two to the Diamonds. It was a massacre.

'*Two* hat-tricks,' cried Dad Savage. 'And both by my lads.'

'Twin hat-tricks by twin strikers,' mused Ratso. 'That's a first.'

'I thought you told us statistics don't matter,' said Liam.

'Did I say that?' asked Ratso. Conor nodded. 'Then I plead temporary insanity. We've got one problem, though.'

'What's that?' asked Liam.

'Well, the scorer of a hat-trick usually gets the match ball. So what do we do with this? You can't share it.'

'Give it here,' said Conor. 'I'll show you what to do with it.' Costello and Brain Damage were wandering disconsolately after their team-mates. Conor targeted Costello carefully with the match ball and caught him smack on the head.

'McGovern!' he bellowed. He was remembering another time when Kev booted the ball into him.

'Not guilty this time,' chuckled Kev.

'Call it pay-back time,' said Conor. 'For Liam's knee and my bike.' Costello was rubbing his head and glaring at Conor.

'Want to make something of it?' asked Liam. Costello gave the twins a long stare then glanced warily at their dad, who was hovering protectively in the background. There was nothing to do but carry on walking.

'Liam,' asked Dad. 'Am I forgiven yet?'

'Sure,' said Liam. 'So long as you take us swimming this afternoon.'

'Come on then, lads,' said Lenny. 'Last one in the pool . . .' he glanced mischievously at Liam, '. . . is a wimp.'

Ten

You never know what you can handle until you have to. For a while there, I thought I was losing it. Just goes to show how strong I can be when I put my mind to it, and let's face it, I had to be. I had my fair share of knocks this time. Mum, for instance, I never thought she'd meet anybody else. I expected her to wait for Dad forever. Stupid, I suppose. Since when did I believe in fairy tales? It makes me sick to think of Mum out with Dougan. Surely it can't last. I mean, a copper! It doesn't change how I feel about her though. Cheryl was right all along. Mum's the best. So she's knocking around with the law. Big deal. After the last couple of years, I can handle just about anything. She's still the same old Mum. I mean, just because he takes her out, it doesn't mean I have to like him. It's not like I'm going to start calling him Dad or anything. Copper will do just fine. No matter what she does or who comes into her life, she'll always be there for me. She lasts.

Same with the Savage brothers. They've just been through a Civil War but when push came to shove, blood was thicker than water. And if they can play like they did on Sunday when they've been ripping bits off each other

*imagine what they can do when things are going for us.
Their partnership up front is a mouth-watering prospect.*

*As for my other problems, they look like carrying on.
There's Dad getting up to mischief right under Dougan's
nose, and that copper's manhunt for another. Let's face it,
this is one kid who's never going to get a taste of the silver
spoon. But who said I was going to have an easy time? Life
threw the gauntlet down to me years ago and I've never
shied away from the challenge.*

*Then there's Costello and Co. It doesn't look like they'll
ever go away. I sometimes think we were made for each
other, created to fight an endless battle. But yes, well, it suits
me. Something tells me that if there was no Costello around
I'd have to invent him. If you're a fighter like me you've got
to have something to fight.*

*Which brings me to the League table. Suddenly it makes
interesting reading.*

	Pl	W	D	L	Pts
Longmoor Celtic	17	11	4	2	37
Ajax Aintree	17	10	5	2	35
Liver Bird	17	10	3	4	33
Rough Diamonds	17	9	3	5	30
Northend United	17	8	6	3	30

*The Cup exit was a disappointment. More than that, it felt
like the end of the world at the time. But we can make up for
it. We can build a new team spirit out of steel and fire. We
can come back and wipe the smile off the Liver Bird's faces.
We're just three points adrift of them and seven away from
the leaders. In a title run-in it's all down to who keeps their
nerve. Longmoor are in pole position now, but nobody likes
having the opposition breathing down your neck. And
when that opposition is as hungry as the Diamonds, they're*

in for a hard time. We can do it. We've got to do it. It's about pride. It's about being a winner. Five games to blaze a trail of glory. Stand by for the final countdown.

Game on.

Other books your might enjoy in the TOTAL
FOOTBALL series

Some You Win . . .

'There's me with my mind full of the beautiful game
. . . and what are we really – a bunch of deadbeats
. . .'

But Kev has a reputation to live up to and when he
takes over as captain of the Rough Diamonds he pulls
the team up from the bottom of the league, and
makes them play to win . . . every match.

Under Pressure

'The pressure's on. Like when you go for a fifty-fifty
ball. Somebody's going to blink, and it isn't me.
Ever.'

Kev, captain of the Rough Diamonds, acts swiftly
when too many of the lads just aren't playing the
game and let pressures off the pitch threaten the
team's future.

Divided We Fall

'If you don't take risks you're nothing. There's only
half an inch of space between determination and dirty
play and I live in it.'

That's the law Kev McGovern lays down for the
Rough Diamonds on the pitch, but what about off it?
When Kev's best mate Jamie's world is wrecked by
dirty play he's desperate to get everything back to
safe, reliable normal.

Injury Time

'Some people have all the luck. Dave Lafferty for one. How else do you explain a kid who's brilliant at everything? I would have given my right arm to swop with Dave.'

But Kev is stunned when he discovers that Dave has to cope with epilepsy. When he suffers a major attack, the victory the Rough Diamonds are so desperate to win, the longed-for junior league challenge cup, hangs precariously in the balance.

Last Man Standing

'Losing's never fun, but sometimes you learn more from a defeat than half a dozen wins'.

John O'Hara is a midfield player for the Diamonds. Kev doesn't know what to do when trouble at home makes John lose form and credibility both on and off the pitch. His mind's just not on the game, and it's up to Kev to get him back on the ball.

Power Play

'What *is* your problem?' asked Kev, starting to lose patience.

My problem thought Chris. 'At the moment . . . you. I want you and your stupid mates to get out of my face.'

The Rough Diamonds are a close-knit team. Kev McGovern makes sure they work hard and play hard. He doesn't make any allowances. That goes for the new boy Chris Power who's just signed up with the

Diamonds. Kev is determined to find out what makes him tick – and he does, but not until the very end, when it's almost too late.

Final Countdown

It looks like Kev 'The Guv'nor' McGovern is leading the Rough Diamonds to a unique league and cup double. He's dreamed of this moment, lived total football and worked his team to the top. But will the ghosts from his past come back to haunt him, ruining all their chances and snatching victory from them?